# THE BELT OF TRUTH
# GENESIS

RICHARD JONATHON CAPUTO

ISBN 978-1-0980-4648-4 (paperback)
ISBN 978-1-0980-4661-3 (hardcover)
ISBN 978-1-0980-4649-1 (digital)

Christian Faith Publishing, Inc.
832 Park Avenue
Meadville, PA 16335
www.christianfaithpublishing.com

Printed in the United States of America

# INTRODUCTION

"IRON SHARPENETH IRON, SO A MAN sharpeneth the countenance of his friend" (Proverbs 27:17).

This book will inevitably divide certain people. Some will claim I have misquoted; others will believe I have overlooked important details. Whatever the assertion may be, this book is not Scripture. It is first and foremost a work of fiction. Furthermore, I strongly believe the Bible's scriptures are so incredibly dense with knowledge, morality, depth, and philosophy that we can dig forever and ultimately miss something profound, whether hidden or in plain sight.

"It is the glory of God to conceal a thing: but the honour of kings is to search out a matter" (Proverbs 25:2).

The pages that follow contain many stories and historical events collected from the Holy Bible. However, the narrative I've constructed is meant to pose a question, an inward question, one in which only the reader can know. And hopefully (depending on the answer), it will provide an opportunity for him/her to examine their own relationship with God.

"Who is he that hideth counsel without knowledge? Therefore have I uttered that I understood not; things too wonderful for me, which I knew not" (Job 42:3).

Whether you are an agnostic, atheist, theologian, scholar, or Christian, welcome! I hope at the very least that you will find this book entertaining and at the very most that these stories pique your interest enough to open the Bible.

"And my speech and my preaching was not with enticing words of man's wisdom, but in demonstration of the Spirit and of power: That your faith should not stand in the wisdom of men, but in the power of God" (1 Corinthians 2:4–5).

# PROLOGUE

# TIME AND POTENTIAL

*THERE ARE NO WORDS* TO DESCRIBE THE paradox of time before time. This concept is so abstract that defining it will require an understanding that can only be found beyond the realm of time itself, an unfathomable idea that can only be properly grasped by those who exist outside of it (John 1:1).

Imagine, if you will, a painting of a man standing in the rain. His face is somber, but little does he know that he's been caught in the moment before he's soaked by the water falling from his broken umbrella.

You look at him. He looks at you. And every time you return to the image, he's still there looking at you looking at him. What we see never changes, but how can we define *his* perspective, especially when we consider that he doesn't even know we exist or that there's anyone watching him at all?

His perception of time, if he has one, differs infinitely from yours and mine. What he considers only an instant, we consider an eternity. And as unlikely as it may seem, this analogy branches outward to the beginning of everything. From him to you, to me, to the Source, time is *relative* and didn't exist any more in the beginning than it does for the man in the portrait.

His painter or his designer or his *creator* did not give him the ability to move within that moment to witness the spectacle of his creation, nor to exist with imperfection and the decay that naturally comes with the constant progression of time. But instead, it's the opposite. This man in the rain under a broken umbrella, alone in an instant, paused for eternity, will only *ever* exist in this moment.

As we examine the image, we also recognize the fact that we don't look at this picture and assume the rain is going upward or that if time *were* present, the man's umbrella will go from broken to functional. We assume a one-way linear progression halted in time but if resumed will result in a very uncomfortable event for our subject. But it doesn't resume. It remains flawless and changeless from the moment of its completion because time *isn't* present. So in this way, he exists forever.

In essence, he is immortal like us. But unlike us, he has no *soul*.

A soul implies something sacred, something gifted (Ecclesiastes 12:7), something to live for. And without a future or a past, what interests, curiosities, or concerns of any significance can this soulless image possibly have?

He was there yesterday, there today, will be there tomorrow and until the end of time. He has no choice, no autonomy, nor free will. He even lacks the necessary knowledge to realize it. Or to be more specific: to realize *at all*.

He'll never know the pain of loss that the future always brings. But he'll never have the cherished past to lose in the first place.

This, of course, begs the question: Is it better that he stay here in this ignorant moment forever? (Job 3:3–26). He has no sense of worry or dread for the water about to cover him nor the weeks of sickness he'll inevitably endure.

Though this may sound an awfully confusing perspective (or lack thereof), we were all there at one point—null, formless, unidentifiable, motionless but never *empty* because He was with us, or to be more precise, we were with Him (Psalm 139:13–16).

Through Him, we existed prior to our existence. His perception is infinite (Psalm 147:5). Ours is finite. And as created beings, unlike Him, time is ultimately what gives *us* purpose.

Hence, like all of God's miracles of creation, time is a *gift*. And like any gift, it carries with it not only opportunity but also the double-edged sword of potential.

It promises heartache, pain, sorrow, anger, loss, regret, disaster, and betrayal. And though it may seem at times like avoiding these circumstances will be ideal, nothing can be further from the truth (Job 42:2–6).

The promised potential of time can *only* exist if it does so through the chaos of free will and the choice to carry on (Proverbs 16:9). Only then can the hierarchies of outcome emerge.

To feel heartache, one must first have the feeling of love. To feel sorrow, one must first have the feeling of happiness. To feel regret, one must have first made a regretful choice.

The difficult times that fall on all of us are referred to as such *because* of our preposition to them and our future potential which would not exist if time flowed any other way.

This is what makes His chosen creation so special—time.

It wasn't the stars or the heavens or the awe-inspiring beauty of the earth, but man that He favored (Genesis 1:26). He willed the separation of light from darkness, and it was good. He pulled the sky from the water, and it was good. He called to life the plants and trees, animals and birds, the sun, the moon, and the stars, and they were good. But it wasn't until the creation of man that He looked upon all His works and saw that it was *very* good (Genesis 1:31).

Give man time, and he will live and love, cherish and hate, create and destroy. And though chaos is inherent in time, so too is the future and all the wonders it can possess. And without the forward momentum of time, there will be no love or laughter, no guilt or pain, no grace or purpose (Ecclesiastes 3:1–8).

An empty prism can only refract its plethora of color when illuminated by a pure and radiant source, eternally immaculate, vibrant, and definitive. Without this light, no rainbow can exist, nor will there be anyone to see it. And like everything else in existence, light moves outward through time from a point of origin (Genesis 9:12–17).

This initial moment, this Genesis, when it all began, was a choice, the first choice, and in it His infinite grace. Knowing all that it meant, He opened His heart, and with four words came everything, "Let there be light."

# CHAPTER ONE

## THE FALL

*THE GARDEN LAY EMPTY* AND VOID OF movement as He stood over the land, looking on in affection for all He had created.

My angelic brethren stood captivated and I with them in the glory unfolding before us. We had come to consciousness on the first day and had witnessed His majesty growing ever more omnipotent with each rising and setting of the sun (Job 38:4–7).

The past five days were tireless (Genesis 2:2), but He knew that His work was almost complete and lacked one final addition, one creation to have dominion over the rest and the last piece in the center of the puzzle before His image could be achieved.

He crouched and pressed His hand to the earth. He closed His eyes and inhaled deeply. So magnificent was this breath that all the waters, trees, and mountains of the earth bowed to Him in praise. Then slowly He arose, and the dirt from the ground swirled up from below His fingers. A whirlwind of dust chaotically flowed upward and out of the ground, collecting in the center of the vortex. Hardening to clay, the core began to grow, smoothing and articulating the figure. His hands shaped it as if operating an invisible potter wheel rolling on its side.

The completed shape floated above the ground. Its molded figure was like a mirror form of its designer. He stood back in testimony. He was satisfied with the result.

The earth split, and a small seam opened, and like sand in an hourglass, the shape fell away, collecting in the crevasse then sealing like a delicate suture.

With a powerful drop, He struck His hand back to the earth, sending a mighty shock wave in all directions, setting right the trees, waters, and mountains.

Then silence.

And a moment later, the dirt began to stir.

First was a hand and an arm that rose up from beneath the ground. Then a foot, a leg, and finally a head and a body.

The dust rolled off the golem, revealing the face of the first man shaped in the image of his Maker. It stood with blank composure, a marionette, neither living nor dead.

The Lord leaned in and touched the manikin's forehead with His own, staring deeply into its vacant eyes as if determining the location of its absent soul. Then finally, He released His breath and exhaled into its nostrils His Holy Spirit—an explosion of consciousness.

The creation shifted, his pupils dilating. Vibrant and beautiful colors filled his eyes, and with a gasp of air, he breathed life for the first time.

In unison, my brethren and I cheered and praised! The cherubim song was filling the airwaves as all of creation had reached completion, and our Lord could finally rest.

Adam was born.

\*\*\*\*\*

The museum was practically empty. Aside from the receptionist and a class of students with their teacher, Gabriel and I were essentially alone. Not that we minded the relatively quiet environment but it did bring forth the speculation that most of those present were not there by choice. Still it was rather odd that in a city this heavily occupied so few would enter such an ornate location.

We had ventured inside on simple curiosity to see what historical moments we could recognize. Sure, it wasn't the Prado or the Sistine Chapel, but it certainly was furnished and elegant. Posters lined the entrance, announcing a gala two weeks past; the upkeep of publicity, unfortunately, was not quite so punctual.

Nevertheless, they had beautiful paintings, sculptures, and recreations spanning across centuries of mankind, an amazing catalog of human accomplishment and progression through time.

Gabriel found the Renaissance tapestries especially intriguing. Many, if not most, were of pagan artists illustrating their false gods of fertility, astrology, and death. Although skillful in their depiction, one could not help but shudder at their message, regardless of its artist's intent.

There were others, however, whose likenesses were strikingly accurate and brought to mind many memories of long since-lived experiences. One piece in particular caught my eye.

It was a tall oil painting hung behind a dusty velvet rope and shielded by thick glass, annoyingly etched and inscribed with graffiti. The plaque at the base of the intricately carved frame read, "Fall of the Morning Star—Unknown."

The image was of a man and woman standing beside a colorful tree, their heads bowed in shame. Their skin was rosy about the cheeks, and the light-green shade of the fig leaves at their waist made them appear mint and freshly plucked. The woman's hand gripped the tail of a black serpent while the man's heel drove into its head with bloodred bite marks on his ankle (Genesis 3:15). Above them was the sun fully eclipsed, a glowing yellow halo emanating from behind it. A comet with a fiery orange face skewed with anguish, shot downward from the sun's center, an undulating streak following its path (Luke 10:18).

"It's been thousands of years, Michael," Gabriel said, joining me in intrigue. "So short were the days of peace, and so long have they been forgotten."

"The day our family was broken." I nodded in agreement.

"Their eagerness became their downfall [Genesis 3:6]," he continued. "And their mortality ignited their ambition. Yet over and over we've fought on their behalf [Psalm 34:7]. For naught, it seems, and I can't help but wonder His purpose and favor for such a simple creation."

"They were manipulated, Gabriel. Their ignorance was a *result* of their purity. We are not much different."

"Indeed, brother, but so imperfect are they that they've forgotten the *origin* of choice, the very thing that provides them with self-determination and even the *option* to be led astray."

"But what is the value of obedience without love? How can they be true and faithful servants if they lack the free will to choose? [2 Peter 3:9]. This is what makes our fallen brother's defiance so disastrous. Our Father loves him like us, but due to his indiscretion, he *himself* cannot reciprocate, and the two became exclusive [Ezekiel 18:23]."

Gabriel thought for a moment, *What a fool.* He shook his head in disgrace.

"Is it possible that He knew?" I added, a seemingly rhetorical question, but he stirred at the conception.

"What do you mean?"

"His actions came at a great and terrible cost, yet I still long for our brother's music [Ezekiel 28:13–15], so pleasing to the ear and touching to the soul. Perhaps it is not our place to know, but I can't help every time the sun sets to ponder with perplexity over his misdeed."

Gabriel seemed to understand my perspective.

"Likewise, brother," he replied. "Jealousy is the wicked mistress of desire."

*****

Adam lived happily with Eve in their paradise in the garden of Eden. Their every want and need was met with abundance, and God's presence sustained them (Genesis 1:29).

Like children, their curiosity kept them busy, and their innocence made them childishly gullible. Their relationship was symbiotic, and their need for each other was essential, not just so one could share experiences with the other but to come together and multiply.

This particular gift was the most unique, considering the physical similarities to their closest cousins, the watchers, or *angels,* as we're more commonly referred to.

Minus our wings, mankind had all of the same features as us and more, as if God had taken the best parts of all His creations and pasted them together with a soul. They looked like us, talked like us, and were loved like us, but they had something we did not, and there were many of us who felt denied as a result.

But none more so than my former brother Lucifer.

Although he loved and worshipped the Lord, he lowered his eyes to Him at the sight of man. He was envious of God's preferential communion with them, like the older sibling to the newborn, and felt somehow ignored as if his Father's attention, which he most desired, was drawn away. But most of all, he despised their simplicity and fragility which churned his distaste toward their ability to procreate.

He believed himself superior to man (Ezekiel 28:14–19), and in so believing, he grew arrogant and spiteful. This assumption manifested a deep and dark hypothesis: If the Lord had made man a lower but more favored creation than the angels in His *own* image, then He *Himself* must be flawed and that he, Lucifer, could see the flaw, thereby setting God's moral authority lower than his own.

He started to convince himself that he was superior, and if only he had the chance, his rule would be a righteous one. He believed that *he* could run things better, that *he* was morally absolute, and that if given the opportunity or the throne, *he would right the wrong*. This poor and miserable logic led ultimately to the point where in his mind, usurping the Lord's power became an obligation of ethics rather than a choice. And he could not rest his conscience until his self-righteous pursuit was claimed, and he attained what he now sought (1 Peter 5:8).

This delusion was not exclusive to Lucifer unfortunately. These feelings had manifested among many of my brothers in heaven, and he was successful in rallying a third of the angels with him in his mutinous rebellion (Revelation 12:4).

That day has burned forever in my mind, a day I only wish I could forget. It was a loss of souls, death, and torment for nothing! Indeed, *a fool* he was on that day. What was once a brilliant musician—a power that stemmed from his gift of sug-gestion—fell away to become nothing more than a mere persuasive salesman of snake oil, a skill he uti-lized for his wretched plot (2 Thessalonians 2:9–10).

My former brother knew that if our Father's heavenly children were to rebel, He would maintain order. So he devised a plan to build his army. But to add to his currently outnumbered ranks, they would have to come from the only intelligent creation that could multiply, God's favored achievement—man (Matthew 13:22).

He took the form of a serpent and went to the youngest of them, Eve, knowing that she had not witnessed the creation in the garden. This made her more naive than her husband and easier to manipu-late (1 Timothy 2:14).

He hid in the grass and waited until Adam was away and she was alone. Then the serpent approached, slithering his way along the path near her.

"Th-th-this garden is full of delicious fruits-s-s," he started. "D-d-did God really tell you not to eat-t-t of them?" (Genesis 3:1).

She looked, intrigued at the talking serpent, having not encountered another speaking creature before, least of all one that slithered on the ground.

"We can eat of any of the trees in the garden except for the tree at its center," she responded. "The tree of the knowledge of good and evil" (Genesis 3:3).

"Th-th-that's rather odd. What makes this-s-s tree any different-t-t?" he asked.

"The Lord said that if we eat of its fruit, we will know death and will be lost and confused," she replied.

"Abs-s-surd!" he hissed. "He *must* know that if you eat of its fruit, the s-s-scales will be lifted from your eyes-s-s, and you will live forever knowing what He knows. He's forbidden it because He's *afraid* of it-t-t as He knows that you will be like Him, a god" (Genesis 3:5).

This was the first lie ever told. It immediately divided man's heart, sending a gap that ran down the center of their conscience, and it still does today. The moment he uttered his false words, the balance in everything was lost. The original moment of doubt was felt. Truth no longer existed exclusively and would have to contend with deceit forever.

Not only did Adam and Eve have access to the tree of life, essentially making them immortal, but they walked side by side with God. Any knowledge they could ever want or need was provided to them by the *source* of all knowledge.

But Eve in her innocence plucked the forbidden fruit from off the branch, and as she bit into it, the serpent, Lucifer, knew he had succeeded in his endeavor. He had usurped the power of the Creator, and nothing would ever be the same. And as Adam arrived, she dropped the fruit, and he realized what she had done.

She had broken the one rule that God had given them, a concept never conceived. It was betrayal through coercion but nevertheless a disobedience to His eternal authority.

Adam looked on in confusion, and a rush of emotion swept over him as his adoration for Eve was insurmountable. Before her, he observed all of God's creation and was unable to find a mate. It was only when the Father took one of Adam's ribs as he slept and used it to form Eve, that he looked upon her and fell in love (Genesis 2:22–24). And at this moment, these feelings rushed forward.

"What have you done?" Adam challenged.

Her expression widened, and fear gripped her. The cosmos in her eyes faded, and her pupils changed from light to dark. The glow that emanated from her aura dimmed until her body was pink, and she trembled in terror. She looked down at her nakedness and felt a desperate and lonely feeling of vulnerability (Genesis 3:7). Then she twisted her body in an attempt to hide herself from her husband's gaze. The original sin had claimed her.

Adam stood in disbelief at what had become of his love hiding herself in a nearby bush. His mind was racked with confusion, culminating to one thought: *What will happen now? God would surely erase her. And I would be left alone again.*

Perhaps his Father would create another mate, and perhaps she would be lovely and pure, but he knew that deep down inside she would not be Eve, and he would long for her forever.

This was a thought he could not bear. Their symbiotic connection was unique and irreplaceable, a connection he was quickly losing, deteriorating before his eyes.

Before he realized it, he had made his choice. He too had plucked a fruit from the tree. And though reluctant, his love overtook him, and he seized his fateful bite.

# CHAPTER TWO

## HERDING THE MOB

*THE BRIGHT AND COLORFUL CITY* SUR-rounded us as Gabriel and I entered the square, a common area at the heart of the city where several main streets converged, marking its location like a treasure map. The buildings were stacked with bill-boards and advertisements. Half-naked men and women danced around on the animated screens, marketing to their respective demographics. It appeared as though the impressive bits of architec-ture were made by a society long forgotten. Now the city's charm was gone, replaced by gluttonous consumerism, leaving much to be desired.

Suddenly, a loud siren rang, and the screens flashed red and black. All the people in the square, in their cars, on their bikes, in their businesses stopped and looked up attentively to the flashing screens as if nothing in their lives was more important than the coming message.

We joined them in intrigue, but our confusion only grew stronger.

The flashing halted, being replaced by a young woman held behind a barrier of glass. The prison's transparent walls were encompassed by small holes, presumably for breathing, not wide enough to slide a pencil through. The young woman's face was bruised and swollen. She had been severely beaten shortly before the broadcast.

The camera panned backward to reveal her shackles and straps firmly holding her in place like a stockade. Then on her left outside the glass enclosure stood the magistrate wearing a long black robe and a curly white wig. His face was covered by a terrifying mask, blank and unfamiliar. The round holes where his eyes should be were void and empty, situated above two dots beneath a small bump in the center of the oblong disguise. Anonymity for this magistrate was clearly of paramount importance to him. In fact, it wasn't exactly clear if he was a *he* at all.

At the bottom of the screen was a timer, sixty seconds, ready to start. Flashing beside the lingering digits were two words, "Vote now!"

The magistrate lifted his hands, palms up, revealing the words *yes* on his right and *no* on his left.

We looked around, baffled in amazement as everyone we could see pulled out their phones and began scrambling to place their entries.

And the timer started.

As more and more submissions were acquired, the magistrate lowered one hand or the other. The woman behind the glass beside him cried and screamed in anticipation of the impending results.

The crowds gathered and shouted, "Do it! Do it! Do it!" with accompanying ovation. Then all in unison they counted down.

"Five." He lifted his right hand.

"Four." He lowered his left hand.

"Three." The crowd stirred.

"Two." The young woman collapsed.

"One." The crowd exploded.

"Zero."

An eruption of cheers filled the air like a tsunami as the timer ran to its conclusion. The people had voted, and they were satisfied with the result.

The magistrate lowered his left hand and pulled a rope with his right, bringing down a massive guillotine, removing the young woman's head in a devastating flash resulting in a geyser of blood.

The shock of such an image being broadcasted so openly overwhelmed us as we turned from the murder taking place before our eyes. But even more unsettling was the crowd. They jumped with ravishment and howled with amusement, overjoyed with their participation in the slaughter like the gladiator arenas so long ago.

"What horrors have they wrought," Gabriel yelled, his voice barely carrying over the horde of citizenry violently singing their victory.

"We must seek counsel from the Lord," I cried back. "This aversion of the law cannot be tolerated!" (John 14:15).

With a bow, the magistrate and the gore faded to black, and text flew over the screen, stopping in the center and flashing, "Guilty. Guilty. Guilty. The defendant has been found guilty of thought crime in the first degree. Sentence is death and erasure from history. All familiar individuals and acquaintances must relinquish any and all evidence of the defendant's existence or share in the ruling of our honored courtroom. This verdict is final and beyond repeal."

Then the screen went black.

The citizens returned to their respective errands and businesses. The commercials flickered back to the billboard screens, and things continued on as normal, as if nothing out of the ordinary had occurred.

Gabriel and I quickly made our leave behind the veil, and as we ascended along the buildings, we crossed an advertisement reading, "Did you miss the verdict? Go to our website and watch it again! Don't forget to vote. It's not just a right. It's a responsibility!"

*****

Cain and Abel were the first real humans as they were the first to be born from man and woman (Genesis 4:1). Their skills and gifts were different, but their individual potentials were commensurate, and it was ultimately their respective dedication that determined their harvest (Genesis 4:7).

Cain, the oldest of the two, worked the land while his younger brother, Abel, was a shepherd. They both put in the hours necessary to yield what they required, but only Abel went beyond the minimum and put real effort into his work.

Upon examination of his brother's production of labor, Cain was overtaken by anger and dejection. The Lord sensed the fire in his eyes and asked, "Why do you burn with enmity and despondency, my son?"

"My brother makes a mockery of my works," he responded. "I present an offering as he did, yet you show him favor over me. Why is my work not worthy of your acknowledgment?"

"Remember, son of Adam," He explained, "the effort you *afford* will decide your yield, however not all things can be earned. Therefore, be mindful, those who desire what they have not produced will be beckoned by sin crouching at their door" (Genesis 4:7).

This assertion only angered Cain further, and his animosity grew with agitation as each day passed. He was not slothful, but he did not strive to better his harvest. Nor could he understand that his works, no matter how good, could ever result in what he sought. He would not allow yesterday to die so that tomorrow could be in any other form than today. And all the while, Abel would, and Cain's frustration would gather greater.

Finally, the hours had accumulated under his brooding, and he reached the threshold of tolerance for his affliction.

While working the land, Cain called to his brother from the field, and as he approached, he tackled him to the ground (Genesis 4:8).

Abel, caught by surprise, was taken down swiftly, a surge of confusion sweeping over him. He pushed, shoved, and writhed about, but his brother would not let him go.

Cain grabbed a nearby rock, heavy enough to require both hands, and lifted it above his head.

The brothers stared into each other's eyes, one set filled with terror, and the other was filled with hatred, an endless moment that seemed to last forever.

Abel's lips quivered and stirred as he attempted to find the words to speak. But before his voice could utter a sound, Cain brought the stone down and struck his brother's head once, twice, then again and again until the movements of Abel's body came to a stop.

The blood dripped and splashed about the soil, drenching the ground beneath them. The earth began to move and shake, sending a massive shock wave outward, as if equilibrium had been broken and balance was lost in response to the now-absent soul ripped away to heaven.

Cain covered Abel's body in dirt to hide what he had done, but the land would not take him and rejected Cain's plight. The earth had birthed the first of man and now was compelled to accept the death of his seed and would not capitulate.

So he covered his slain brother with stones that he might escape punishment, never fully realizing the horrible act he had committed, the true destruction of innocence, the first murder.

Thinking himself vindicated and alone in his knowledge, he returned home carrying nothing but apathy. But the Father was waiting as he arrived.

He entered to see his mother on her knees crying out, his father beside her.

He didn't know how, but they knew.

"Cain," the Lord said, "where is Abel, your younger brother?" (Genesis 4:9).

"How should I know?" he replied callously. "Am I my brother's keeper?"

"You seek to deceive your almighty Father?" God replied. "The blood of your brother cries out to Me from the ground! You have defiled My gift to you, and the land will no longer receive your efforts" (Genesis 4:12).

His voice was stern but filled with grief. Cain's action was the first of its kind, and now His creation was tainted beyond repair.

"You will wander restlessly on the earth for the remainder of your days!" He continued. "As you have violated the land, so too shall it bear you no accord."

Cain dropped to his knees in surrender. "Please, Lord, your punishment is too great! Everyone will know what I have done and how I've fallen from your graces. They will harass and attack me, and those who pass me will surely kill me!" (Genesis 4:13–14).

The Lord took pity as He looked upon the child of man, but He was tormented by what he had done. An imbalance had been established, and the earth would be forever changed. He reached out his hand and touched Cain's forehead. Heat emanated from his fingertip, burning his skin, and a mark was formed, a shape to recognize and avoid for those who wish to bring death upon the first offspring of His beloved creation (Genesis 4:15).

"Whosoever sees this mark will know of what you have done. They will hate and ridicule you. They will throw stones to harm and maim you, but they will not kill you. For if they do, they will suffer My vengeance seven times over."

And He cast him out, never to return.

# Chapter Three

# Covenant and Prophecy

*THE EARTH GREW DISTANT*, AND THE lights speckled off its surface as we approached the heavens. We could hear the cherubim singing their never-ending praises, glorious and beautiful, sending a current of elation rippling through the kingdom. Like a choir of all the birds in the sky and fish in the ocean and beast on the land joined together and sang in harmonious unison, an immutable sound which was heard since the dawn of time but never aged in beauty (Isaiah 6:1–4).

We flew above the crystal river toward the source of the stream where the Lord sits upon His eternal throne. The eastern sky was ablaze with white glistening colors of rose and azure dancing their way like notes on sheet music across the sky to the west and becoming emerald and violet. The cities surrounding the castle were of polished gold, shining our reflections back at us as we glided onward (Revelation 21:21). The castle itself, magnificent beyond all words, was lined with ruby and sapphire and all the colors of the rainbow and more. Warmth radiated through the translucent walls, pulsating with euphoric light as we made our landing.

We approached the throne and bent our knees, lowering our heads in reverence and praise, His breathtaking presence overwhelming us, as always.

"Michael? Gabriel?" the Almighty asked. "To what do I owe the gift of your visit?"

"My Lord, we have come to seek the counsel of your Word," I responded. "That we might know His judgment and follow Your will."

I turned to Gabriel and gestured for him to continue.

"Almighty Father," Gabriel explained, "we have come from the land of your favored creation where we witnessed a great atrocity, an execution so vile and so public, the likes of which we've never seen. The whole city was turning their attention to witness it. And the people cheered and widely participated in the wickedness, as if their lives were void of meaning and emptiness embodied them."

"I see," said the Lord. "Perhaps the time is upon us."

His breath fanned the back of my neck as if I were kneeling before a mighty lion, and I could feel his Holy Spirit flow through me. A comfort so endearing, it could only be found in awe and grace through submission and surrender, a feeling of ease like a warm blanket in the cold desert or the relief found in shelter from a great storm.

"Return to the earth, my sons," He continued, "and walk amongst them for forty days and forty nights. Do not seek the wicked but instead seek the righteous. Take with you this measure and record all that you find. And when you return to Us, We will inform you of Our judgment."

His Word kissed my ear, and I bowed and gave Him worship, as likewise did Gabriel beside me. I reached out my hands and received His divine tool. Then we stood and made our leave back to the world of man. Drifting away from the comfort of his presence, even in heaven, can leave one wanting.

I looked upon the measure issued by the Lord. It was long like a scepter, solid gold and weighty, lined along its staff with numbers currently resting on a long string of zeros. I pressed my thumb across a groove in the hilt, and the staff retracted like a turtle to its shell, making it compact and easy to carry.

And as Gabriel and I descended through the heavens with the song of the cherubim growing weaker, my heart sank, and my eyes were heavy. I was not optimistic for our return.

*****

There were many times throughout the ages that God imparted wisdom (James 1:5). There were times when He showed great visions to the righteous and prophecies to the worthy (2 Peter 1:21), times where He sent us down on His behalf both in salvation and in judgment (Genesis 19:16); there were even times where He walked side by side with His elect, living their experiences with them (Genesis 18). Although seldom and few may be recorded, the examples of His presence, His providence, and His glory exist in all of us.

But there were rare occasions when the Lord commanded it that a man would be brought to *us* to witness in the heavens, and their extraordinary journey was to be kept as a record on the earth.

The first of these phenomena was entrusted to Enoch (Genesis 5:24), and of all the stories passed down to this day, his was the most disputed.

God was the beginning of all things, and although His *only begotten* Son would not be born on earth for thousands of years, His *earthborn* son too was a son of God (Luke 3:38).

Adam was the first man, and as such, he was named accordingly, as Adam means *man* formed from the dust of the earth.

Adam and Eve's third son, who was gifted from God after the death of Abel, was to bring about a new nation of untarnished men. And as such, he was named Seth, or *appointed* (Genesis 4:25).

Then Seth had a son and named him Enosh. It was in his time that man began to blaspheme the name of our living God, and so he was named *mortal man* (Genesis 4:26).

Then Enosh had a son and named him Kenan, for his birth marked a time of great *sorrow*.

Kenan would have a son, Mahalalel, and so named him *blessed god*.

And Mahalalel would have Jared as his son, meaning *shall come down*.

Then Jared would father Enoch. His time on earth was shorter than that of his father and that of his own after him, but his *teachings* would be proof of all the coming times (Hebrews 11:5).

Furthermore, Enoch would father Methuselah who would become the oldest man who ever lived, and upon *his death shall bring* the great judgment soon to come.

Methuselah's son was named Lamech, as his time was of great *despairing*.

And finally, Lamech would father Noah. And it was in his time *comfort and rest* would come to the earth from all her aches and pains.

Why was this so important?

If you knew these stories already, this might not surprise you at all. But those who were not familiar with the inner workings, the behind-the-scene effects, the providential significance of our God's ever-amazing grace were often overcome with the mind of a child witnessing a coin appear behind their ear.

This was not only a record of genealogy or a way to link one historical figure to another.

This was a prophecy, arguably the first prophecy.

It was told through the names of the line of Adam to Noah.

And as such, it was a miracle from God to his people to warn those before, to prepare those during, and to remind those after: He is the Most High, and He loves His creation.

The god-man is *appointed.* A *mortal man* of *sorrow* is born. The *blessed god shall come down, teaching* that his *death shall bring* those in *despair comfort and rest.* Amen.

\*\*\*\*\*

I came to Enoch in the twilight hour on a mission of great importance. He was a man three hundred years old with grown sons yet still spry with a touch of youth, which kept him eager and curious. As always, he was writing, his memoir near finished, never knowing he would soon have much more to record. His candle flickered on his desk as I appeared to him.

"Enoch," I said, "take my hand and come with me, and I will show you all that God has promised for this world and the next" (Enoch 1:2).

He trembled and knelt, averting his eyes. Taking my arrival with hesitancy, he seemed to recognize my face, although we had never met.

"Do not turn away, son of Jared," I continued. "Your eyes will witness many things that should blind another man. But the Lord has gifted you with sight beyond sight that you may tell of what you have seen."

He lifted his head, and our eyes met, and even I was struck with astonishment at their beauty.

His irises were that of the earth, and his pupils were that of heaven. His corneas were like the sea between the stars, and the outer lenses were translucent but perfectly reflective.

These eyes were designed to see beyond the veil, beyond time.

I reached out and grabbed hold of his wrist, and we shot into the sky to begin our journey.

\*\*\*\*\*

The wonders and terrors that we witnessed that night would burn behind my eyes forever as well as the visions of a calamity that split the heavens by a third and those that followed my fallen brother, and they were like nightmares (Enoch 1:5).

They shook the earth and its foundation and built an army of giants. These mammoth creatures were born of the earthly women but planted by the seeds of the fallen ones, an abomination under God of the union between eternal angels and man. They were known as the Nephilim (Enoch 7:1–6, Genesis 6:4).

Their hunger was great as they devoured all the animals and harvests but found they could not be satisfied, and soon they craved the blood of man (Enoch 7:4).

Many of God's children would meet their end by way of the appetites of the giants and their insatiable lust for dominion. And the blood of man soaked deep into the soil of the earth (Enoch 9:9).

So detestable and wicked were the Nephilim that even their lusts of the flesh were sour. And they began to take to bed the animals of the earth and of the sky and make of them their concubines. Their offspring would be the bane of the earth and all her land, stripping the life from all that could be found, leaving it gray and desolate and without color. These anathemas were known as the Chimera. And they too were an affront to God (Enoch 7:5).

Then we looked upon a man, humble and pure, and I beheld myself beside him, whispering in his ear (Enoch 10:1–3). The man built up a mighty ark to preserve the line of Adam and all the innocence of creation that remained. Suddenly, the earth filled to the sky with water, rinsing clean the abhorrence from the land.

Then the water washed away. There was peace upon the earth, and man had many generations. But before long, the men became wicked once more.

And it was then that we saw the Son of Man, the great Logos, the Lamb of God appear, and the gates of heaven flew open. The righteous of the earth were pulled up to the heavens, and the wicked were smote in a blaze of fire (Enoch 48:1–10).

And so the earth was made new again, and His kingdom will reign forever.

*****

We returned a moment later, as if we had never left, the visions and prophecies echoing off of Enoch's eyes. We had been shown many things of the past, of the present, and of the future yet to come, and he had only a brief time to catalogue and teach these commencements.

"Go now, Enoch," I told him. "Record this journey tonight and witness to your family. For I will return to you tomorrow at dusk and claim you yet again. Say your peace and hug your sons. You will not return to the earth" (Enoch 83).

Enoch did as he was told, and when I returned to take him, he came readily and was never seen on earth again.

# Chapter Four

# The Flood

*THE DUST FLEW UP,* AND THE SMOKE bellowed as the bombs exploded around us. We had decided to start our journey in the land once settled by the sons of Adam after the fall in the land of Babylon, now known as Iraq. This decision did not bode well.

To the north were the mountains of Ararat where Noah's ark landed after the flood (Genesis 8:4). And to the west was a fallen structure, a monument to remember those who sought to reach the heavens by their own means and their ultimate failure and disbursement (Genesis 11:5–9).

The region had seen many dynasties of mankind, and as a result, it had been built up and torn down several times over. This, apparently, was still an ongoing issue.

The people had been led astray through their idolatry, worshipping false gods, and even to this day would struggle making war over the land, a land they had confused as the location of the garden.

Some of these men were liars, and some of them were not, but all these men simply failed to realize that Eden was never *on* the earth but above it (Genesis 2:8–14). And although Adam and Eve settled here after their fall from grace, no man would ever in life achieve the paradise again, for the Lord knew that man was born unto sin and could not be granted access to the tree of life as in doing so would condemn mankind to their eternal folly (Genesis 3:22).

We stood in the center of the destruction taking place. The air snapped and whistled from the hail of gunfire surrounding us. The buildings and structures were in shambles, barely standing, and the air was thick with the smell of death and destruction. Sound waves of lamentations of women and children were drowned out by the onslaught and the war cries of men.

A small hand gripped my sleeve. I looked down to see the face of a child, her innocence buried beneath the dirt and tears dried and hardened over her once-soft skin. She pointed to a nearby structure hidden under rubble and pulled with haste on my arm.

Gabriel and I followed her, ducking under the broken awning and entering the shelter. It was safe for now, but my fears for the child only strengthened.

In the tiny sanctuary were two fractured families, amounting to less than one. The young girl was now huddled in the corner; two young boys were holding rifles, the younger of the two with a bloodied bandage around his arm, and there was an old woman who received us with distress and frustration.

"What were you fools doing standing out there?" the old woman asked. "The eye of the storm is passing us now. If you'd stood there any longer, you would've been killed!"

She carried herself with a limp under her long black robe that ran the length of her frame to her head. She shuffled over to Gabriel, hunched over her cane, bearing the weight of her broken body. She looked at him for a moment then swung her hand and slapped his face.

"This young girl lost her whole family yesterday and yet risked her life for you!" she continued. "Have you nothing to say?"

"My apologies," he responded. "We had only just arrived and were unaware of the bloodshed taking place."

Baffled by his response, she took a step back, as if contemplating whether or not to slap him again.

"You must not have come from *outside* the city," she continued, "since no one with eyes and ears would enter this war zone willingly, at least not with a sound mind as the devastation can be seen for *miles*. Where on earth did you come from?"

Before I could answer, she shook her head (no doubt assuming us to be in shock or unfit mentally) and limped back to her makeshift bed. Her youngest grandson laid his head on her lap as she sat. They did not have many amenities, and their sanctuary was far from pleasant, to say the least. Yet we could tell they had been here for days.

We studied the faces of our company. Aside from the old woman, none were older than a decade. Their eyes were empty, void of love, with haunting visions filling them, constantly revisiting the horrors they had witnessed. But they dared not remember the comfort of their mothers or the faces of their fathers as doing so would break them.

They remained cold and hard, burying their pain deep below the surface, a way to endure through the ongoing fight, not as a guarantee of survival but as their only chance to stay grounded in reality and not fall to pieces under sorrow.

I stood and approached the young girl, who sat trembling, her head in her arms wrapped tightly around her knees. She wept in silence, like that of a mouse, feeling lost and alone with nothing left to live for. I laid my hand upon her shoulder, and she was startled, peering up at me through polished diamonds of topaz situated roughly amongst the dried gravel and soot.

"Thank you for your kind act of heroism," I said. "Strong and patient is the will of God. And if you so wish it, you too will be welcomed into his kingdom" (Romans 10:9).

Her eyes began to twinkle, and I could see the hope still buried deep behind the dirt and tears.

"God?" The moment was broken by the oldest of the young boys. "Is this the God who took my father from me and who caused the evil men from across the ocean to enter my father's home uninvited? Is it He who allowed the demons to take my mother and sister as they cried out to Him in anguish? There is no mercy to be had from our God. He possesses no concern for His people!"

He paused for a moment to drive home his point.

"Look here at my brother," he continued, "only seven years old. He was shot in the arm trying to protect his sister, only to watch her die a moment later. Your God is real, but He is *not* loving. I only wish He did not exist at all so that we might avoid His terrible fury" (Job 2:9).

To hear such irreverence from the mouth of a child struck me to my core. Their short and dreadful lives thus far were beyond the reach of their control. Their anguish was great and their suffering unworthy. Many were they that feared our God, but few were they that loved Him (John 14:21).

I reached into my robes and pulled out the measure then held it before him to see. I depressed the groove of the hilt, and it shot out to its full length. The numbers were bright with light and spinning like the dial of a scale after a heavy stone is dropped on its spring-loaded surface.

"This measure is a tool from the almighty God," I replied. "It has been bestowed upon me and my brother to weigh the righteous of the earth."

He looked at the solid-gold staff with awe and amazement, running his fingers across the intricate embroidery. Its glow was flooding the empty room with orange-and-brown light.

The numbers slowed their count and stopped:
000,077
It had calculated the number of those deemed worthy from all the men, all the women, all the children, all the souls that struggled through hardship, and less than a hundred could be found in the city. And as I looked upon the faces around us, I prayed that they would be included in its number.

*****

One tribe now claimed dominion over all, and those who did not join their ranks would be devoured by them. This tribe's leader was a ruthless tyrant who ruled with fear, and the destruction he wrought burned the land asunder, a direct descendant of the murderer Cain.

His name was Tubal-Cain (Genesis 4:22).

He had amassed a powerful kingdom, and after his father met his gruesome end in the talon of a monstrous dragon, he spent his life hunting and slaughtering the Nephilim and their wicked offspring. He carried nothing with him but bloodlust and his army of followers. Many of whom shared his thirst for death and destruction, but those that didn't met their swift end by one way or the other.

Tubal-Cain and his ilk had slaughtered many abominations from the earth, but he would not rest until all were dead, and he took what he desired.

However, there was one among them that still walked under God, and Tubal-Cain had yet to find.

His name was Noah (Genesis 6:9).

Noah, like his great-grandfather, was favored by God. And similarly, I was sent to commune with him.

The sun was low, and the morning just began as I reached Noah's side. He sat with his eyes closed in meditation, a basket of berries beside him. I was not to allow him to see my presence as his *faith* would determine the future of mankind (Hebrews 11:7).

Leaning in, I began to whisper, not words but visions, and his mind lit up like a birthing star:

He stood before his grandfather Methuselah who lay old and dying from almost a century of age (Genesis 5:27). Their eyes locked, and he smiled at his grandson. Then he closed them and died. A moment later, a geyser of water shot up from beneath him, and Noah was swallowed in the deluge. Fighting and kicking, he reached for the surface under miles of water. All around him were animals, birds, giants, and men floating lifeless, crushed and drowned in the sea above the mountains.

Then below the death lining the seafloor, two by two, the animals rose up. And as his eyes followed their ascension to the surface above him, a massive wooden structure silhouetting the sun opened widely to receive them.

And he woke.

*****

We waited for the children to fall asleep then nodded to the old woman in appreciation and exited the hideout. The fighting had ceased about an hour ago, but much time had been wasted in our waiting. We looked around carefully before extending our wings. We needed to hurry, and we could not afford to walk the streets in the darkness, and so we slipped behind the veil to remain undetected. The measure was safely packed away.

The cities and towns below us had many more like the ones we met, unfortunate bystanders in a deadly war that pillaged their homes and killed their families. As we soared above them, some were added to the count, and many were not, but our quest was only beginning.

We moved west until we reached the coast, flying directly over the synagogues where Christ had taught then followed his path south through Jerusalem (Matthew 4:23). I had hoped to see more evidence of His teachings, but they appeared to have been destroyed decades earlier.

We continued west at the Gulf of Aqaba then over Egypt, passing the pyramids in Giza. The Sphinx was watching the direction of our approach as we flew over the Nile. The desert was vast and empty, not exactly the best place to find anything, least of all the souls of the righteous. However, I remembered a large city near the ocean, heavily pop-ulated, and I was sure it would be a good place to stop.

Before we could reach it, however, we halted our path at a peculiar site in northern Libya in the mouth of the Mediterranean Sea.

There were boats lining the harbor miles out, awaiting their turn to dock. Those which departed had many more passengers than those which were arriving, another example of the corruption in the hearts and minds of mankind.

Somehow, the act of slavery—abolished worldwide centuries ago—had reestablished itself in the region. This disgusting practice was often referenced in our Lord's holy book but was just as often misunderstood. In those days, there were few on the earth, and those that lacked resources could give their lives unto servitude to survive. A servant was not a slave in the modern sense of the word (Luke 22:26). Servants had autonomy and were often added to the family of those they served. Slaves, however, had no freedom due to a wicked idea of genetic inferiority. This region should know, more than anywhere else, what He will do to free His people (Exodus 21:24).

I was caught by surprise as Gabriel was no longer beside me and had begun diving toward the port. I flew to catch him up, but he had already landed, depressing the earth, creating a massive earthquake. Then he shot back into the sky and readied himself for another dive.

"Gabriel!" I shouted. "We are not to interfere, brother!"

"How can we stand and do nothing?" he responded with emotion. "They've returned to the barbarism once abolished by our Father. I don't know if I have the strength to repeat what He asked of me in Egypt. I cannot kill children again" (Exodus 12:12).

The ground swelled from his attack, and the tide curled, taking multiple ships down to the water's depths. The people screamed and cried in horror while those in chains dropped to their knees and prayed, not in terror for their lives but thanks unto God, for to them, this end was better than where they were headed.

"Go and release them," the Lord whispered in my ear.

I turned to Gabriel, who too received His message, and we descended. Quickly, I gathered them, breaking the chains on their hands while my brother collected a vessel. We boarded them as the earthquake subsided and pointed them north to the island of Malta.

"Do not turn back, and do not return," I told them. "Upon your arrival, take heed of those who help you, and do not accept assistance without reciprocation [2 Corinthians 9:6]. Those who do not respect the land that takes them in will bring the horrors they fled from, and this cancer will spread."

Then we disappeared from them. And as we shot over the waters going north toward Europe, I glanced at the measure:

001,414

*****

Methuselah sat alone on his mountain, watching the sky flitter and flow like schools of colored fish in a stream. Years had passed since he had conversed with his grandson, and knowing his time drew near, he decided to look upon him and deliver his final blessing.

Noah had been hard at work since receiving his commission, and his ark was near completion. He had heard the message the Lord had delivered through me and was diligent in his response. Nevertheless, his grandfather's visit brought him joy and comfort.

Shem was the first to see his great-grandfather's approach as he was out collecting the last of the food they needed as rations for the long journey.

"Shem, my boy," shouted Methuselah, "you've become quite the grown man!"

"Great-grandfather!" he responded. "What a fantastic surprise. My father will be most pleased."

Shem ran to Methuselah's side, offering support on his arm, and walked with him to the ark. The first two levels' doors were sealed, leaving only the third open. And standing before it was Noah, six hundred years old, his long beard thrown over his shoulder (Genesis 7:6). He came down and embraced his grandfather, and they spent the day in fellowship.

"The time is upon us, Noah." Methuselah's eyes passed over his family. "The rain will soon be on the land, and your journey will begin."

"We're almost done, Grandfather," Noah replied. "We had just finished applying the last of the pitch, and God willing, she will float. Our ark's bottom two floors are filled with the animals and beasts of the land and trees. All that we await are the aviaries to fill the third."

Methuselah cracked a smile and pointed ahead of him to the south. Noah and his sons turned to see the sky speckled with a thin black sheet moving toward them and casting a long shadow. The tweets and chirps and crows and whistles filled the airwaves as the birds flew in and made their nests on the ark.

"It appears you have arrived just in t—" Noah turned back to his grandfather, only to see he was gone.

The wind kicked up around them, and they stood as the casks of water fell.

Noah grabbed his sons and shouted, "Go into the ark! The rain is upon us. We haven't got much time!"

His sons all ran to meet their wives in the ark, but Noah was not with them.

"Where is Father?" cried Japheth.

"Look!" Ham pointed to the ground at the ark's base, and there stood his father face-to-face with an army of men.

Lining the front of the massive army were a scourge of wicked beasts and giants. Bound and chained to the submission of their masters.

One man in front approached Noah, carrying a potent air of pretension.

"Son of Seth," he shouted, "it is I, Tubal-Cain, your king. We have learned of the Creator's plan and will not lay down our lives to Him without a fight. I have been watching you, and I know you have collected plenty of food and livestock. Your vessel is grand and has much room that can hold us. I come with an offer."

Noah stood strong and unmoved; regardless of the cost, he would not give them an inch.

"Allow us to board and share in salvation," he continued, "or be removed by force and die."

Still Noah gave no acknowledgment of Tubal-Cain or his foolish proposal, for he knew the Lord's plan would not be averted.

"Son of Cain," Noah started, "you have made your bed one of death and destruction, and the time has come for you to lie in it" (Psalm 2).

He backed away and scaled the ark, joining his family inside.

"So be it." Tubal-Cain turned and joined his army. "My brothers, this man holds the keys to your survival. Are you going to let him walk away with them? Or do you want to live?"

They cheered and threw their hands in the air then began to charge the entrance. But before they could reach it, the ground split open all around, and a fountain of water shot the ark to the air from the floodgates below (Genesis 7:11). My brothers and I were beneath the surface, breaking the seals on the fountains of the deep. And as so often happens, the Lord's timing was impeccable. Like lighting, Gabriel reached the ark and spread his wings wider than I had ever seen. Spiraling through the typhoon, he led the ark to safety above the cataclysm below. With such grace and delicacy did the ark fly that the animals were rocked to sleep, and the Lord shut them in. Yet with such force were the waters in the earth released that all the men, the Nephilim, the beasts, and the birds outside the ark were frozen in place and crushed.

Several months passed and in search of land, Noah released a raven, my brother, who flew to and fro but did not return (Genesis 8:7). Then he released a dove, His Son, and he returned with an olive branch (Genesis 8:10–11). And as a shadow of things to come, it was then that the doors of the ark were opened, and the sun looked upon him with warmth.

# CHAPTER FIVE

## CONCEIVING THE ANATHEMA

*SEVERAL DAYS HAD PASSED,* AND THE measure was slowly counting. I couldn't help but wonder what number would be enough. There were billions of lives on earth today, but how many of them are worthy?

I remembered the past and the times He revealed His judgment and came to the conclusion that perhaps 10 percent would be sufficient, but of course, this was only speculation. Even still, 1 percent seemed almost unreachable at hundreds of millions of souls.

I shook it off and decided not to worry since I knew deep down that only He would know the answer (Romans 10:6–7).

We had passed through Gaul, now known as France, and headed inland from the tower near the coast to Geneva at the southern tip of Gomer or Germany today.

The people had amassed from all over the world to a massive convention, unveiling new technologies and concepts. These new advancements showcased mankind's affinity to build and design great and wonderful creations for transportation. In the years passed, they had revealed new ideas for cars and planes to move them farther and faster throughout the earth. But this year was different.

Cars were still prominent, but the new concepts were in their usage. After implementing their ideas for autonomous vehicles, the next step would be getting their customers to their respective locations without one at all.

They called it Bohu-Dalet Technology. Built on the back of their previous accomplishments in quantum computing and particle acceleration. And much like its technological predecessors, carried an ironic, yet strikingly descriptive name and symbolic label.

This new invention, if implemented, would give men access to a doorway from one location to another anywhere in the world. But of course (as always), they failed to realize that in doing so, they had opened up a portal to the demonic realm.

This technology was developed over many decades by top scientists around the world. Their goal was valid, but their earnest nature blinded their reason with curiosity (James 1:14–15).

And so we flew past them and onward as our commission was to seek the *righteous*.

*****

Noah had grown old and tired as the years came and went. He had made a beautiful vineyard at the foot of the mountain blessed by God's bow in the sky (Genesis 9:12–13). But he was often sorrowful for the loss of life he had witnessed. This avocation kept him busy in body but not in mind, and he often would become drunk with wine in an effort to bury his grief.

One night while intoxicated, he sealed himself in his tent and removed his clothes to feel as Adam did (Genesis 2:25). But the wine took him, and he fell asleep naked.

Ham was nearby and went to fetch his father for the night but laughed in surprise at the sight of him. He then went to his brothers and told them, mocking Noah in his drunkenness (Genesis 9:22–23).

Shem and Japheth took a blanket with them to their father and walked backward to avoid looking upon him as they covered him.

As Noah awoke, he saw what had happened and cursed Ham for his insolence.

"You and your son Canaan will be cursed!" Noah declared. "He will serve at the feet of his brothers. But Shem and Japheth will have sons, and they will receive the Lord's praise" (Genesis 9:24–27).

Many decades would pass, and Ham would have many more sons, as would his brothers. The first of which was Cush, whose son would name his land after his father. The land of Cush at that time became popular and flourished with great progressions of science.

Nimrod, Cush's son, Ham's grandson, was the spearhead of their advancements (Genesis 10:8–12). There was no barrier of language in those days as all who lived had come from the ark. This made the eagerness to grow unanimous.

"Come all ye people," Nimrod proclaimed. "And let us build a great tower, one to reach the heavens and show that we too are as great as our Creator!" (Genesis 11:3–4).

And so they built it, and the Lord responded in kind.

Darkness fell on the land of Cush, and all inhabitants were afflicted with sleep. He sent me down with Gabriel, and we went room by room and whispered in their ears one by one, planting seeds of confusion in their minds. Then we left and with us the night, waking them from their slumber. When they tried to speak, they could no longer be understood as the languages in their minds had been changed. Thus the land could no longer carry its name as no one could properly speak it, and it became known as Babylon (Genesis 11:5–9).

Then all the people left the land and dispersed to form other nations, and the tower was abandoned.

\*\*\*\*\*

Our route continued to the east over many countries, all of which contained signs and wonders, their meanings lost to time and often misunderstood. From the Maykop to the Cimmerians, the Baodun to the Yueshi, ancient cultures and traditions lay in ruin to remind those of a time before the flood.

Several of Christ's apostles would traverse these lands, and in so doing, they would meet their ends at the hands of unbelievers. Even some who did believe fell prey to the power of their pride, causing generations of bloodshed and servitude in the name of God, foolishly breaking the Lord's commandments (Exodus 20:1–17) and condemning their souls to the eternal fire.

Nevertheless, these lands were filled with men, believers of the Word and otherwise, who lived under rulers and tyrants, and the manifestations of their tyranny was holding what should be free people under duress of criminality or so as they poorly defined it.

These people had accepted a system of governance, structured by a lifelong accumulation of social interaction. What they buy and sell, who their family and friends are, what they do with their free time and at work—all of these interactions and more are collected in a database and used to determine their position in the hierarchy. Their *score* will ensure they and their posterity live in poverty or riches, fame or ostracism, freedom or enslavement forever, a system rife with corruption from its inception.

This system wasn't the worst of this land's problems. In fact, the most immediate issue was glaring; the toxic air that filled the atmosphere in this region was so dense. One could hardly see through it at all, let alone breathe it, a result of chemical malpractice and disregard for the now-fragile environment denigrated by the very people who inhabit it.

Twenty days had already passed on our mission. We had reached the halfway point, and the measure had collected less than forty thousand. My worst fears were beginning to manifest.

We continued our travels south over Indonesia into Australia where we added several thousand more to the count. Then we continued east over the Pacific and into South America.

Working our way from south to north, from Argentina to Brazil then from Colombia to Venezuela, it was here that we collected the most so far and where we decided to rest.

*****

The sky was fully immersed in darkness as we landed down. There were no people in sight, making our descent and entry light but our guard and caution heavy. The street was littered with garbage and strewn about as if it had been rifled through days ago and only the paper and waste remained.

None of the streetlights were in operation, nor were there any pedestrians or cars to use them. Many of the businesses were boarded up and seemingly abandoned while the others were closed and barred. It was oddly quiet.

"Where is everyone?" Gabriel inquired.

A figure shifted in the distance and caught my eye from over his shoulder, scattering quickly into a nearby alley, the sound of bottles and cans dropping behind it.

We turned and followed the sound.

The alleyway was too dark to see down, and neither of us was in the particular mood for a rude awakening.

"After you." I gestured to Gabriel.

"I insist." He waved humorously.

Suddenly the dark figure leapt out from behind the empty dumpster and charged in our direction.

With remarkable speed, Gabriel snatched the aggressor by the neck and held it in place.

It was a young woman no older than thirty. Her hair had matted to the point of dreading, and her face was so heavily covered in grime that she resembled a beast more than a woman.

"*Liberame!*" she shouted. "I won't go back! You can't make me!"

"Be calm." I reached out my hand and passed it over her head to ease her wild temperament. Her body went slack, and Gabriel slowly released her.

"Why do you hide in the shadows?" he asked.

"Don't mock me, gestapo. I know about your curfew."

"We are not who you think, child," I responded. "We only just arrived. Tell me, what has happened here?"

She seemed confused, as if such a question was absurd.

"*Tonto!* How do I answer a question like that?" she responded. "Where do I even begin?"

"At the beginning," Gabriel added.

This only seemed to confuse her more.

"Where did you say you were from?" she inquired.

"We're from somewhere far from here. We're on a mission of grave importance, and we're running out of time. Please tell us. Where are all the people?"

"Not here," she whispered. "We can't stay outside. They'll be here soon, and when they find us, they'll…please… I know a place."

We followed her through the deserted city, staying close to the shadows. The eerie silence was only broken by the intermittent passing of pattering feet on concrete and the following sirens that pursued them, each time tucking quietly back into a pitch-dark alleyway for cover.

Eventually, we reached the young woman's destination, a small hideaway above the river of sewage (where they excavate daily for scraps of silver and gold) conveniently hidden by a broken piece from the bridge above.

She was not alone here. Her community consisted of several others mostly her age and younger as well as bugs and insects resting on beds of damp cardboard and garbage. The utterly pathetic conditions were made especially appalling by the stench of human waste bellowing from the waters below them. Nothing could have prepared us for the smell, which (oddly enough) no one else seemed to even notice.

"Is this where you live?" I asked, my concern impossible to hide.

"Yes," she responded. "This has become our only place of refuge."

"From what?" Gabriel added.

"From the gestapo, *el jefe*, the man." She sat on the edge overlooking the river, her feet dangling carelessly mere meters from the putrid waters below. "Many years ago, our *gobierno* changed, and everything fell apart. First it was our weapons. Then it was our freedoms. Then it was our food. It happened so fast. I don't think anyone knew what they were asking for."

"I don't understand," Gabriel interjected. "What could cause such terrible living conditions in a region so lush with natural resources?"

"It's simple, *tonto*. We wanted free education, free health care, free food, free housing. We wanted everything free. But people don't understand that nothing is free, especially when you ask *el gobierno*. All they want is power, and when they get it, all they want is more."

"Why not fight? Why not take back your freedom?" I asked.

"Ha ha," she laughed violently. "You...you think me and my starving *camaradas* can take on the well-fed, well-armed, well-funded armies of *el gobierno*? They would clean the sewers of our stench before we could step one foot onto *la capital*. You think we live here because we like it or they can't find us? They know where we are. Does a man stop to kill the intrusion of cockroaches while passing by the gutter? It's the smell that keeps them from here. This is not a battle we can win. This is a war we've already lost."

The night grew deeper, and the young woman and her company had fallen asleep, so Gabriel and I took our leave. We continued into the North American continent and collected many souls as we flew over the southern region and into America. The measure had become quite burdensome, and I handed it to Gabriel to carry. This mission was seemingly more and more futile as each day passed, and the weight of my conscience was beginning to be too heavy for me to bear. Perhaps our God knew this. Perhaps He had given me this challenge to test my character, perhaps not. My heart was broken for these fallen people. So lost were they as to be completely unaware of the fate yet to befall them.

Nevertheless, I would carry on. My brother and I had never fallen short of the command of our Lord, and we certainly wouldn't start now. I would put my faith in my Father in heaven, and His Word would be my strength. And as the sun would rise on a new day and kiss my cheek, I would be renewed. And my sorrow, although great and heavy, was outweighed by my faith and determination as we yet again approached the next city.

# Chapter Six

## A Meaning to Life

*I REMEMBER A SIMPLER TIME*—A TIME when a man would wake with the dawn and enjoy the sunrise before a hard but worthwhile day of labor (Colossians 3:23), not laboring for someone else but so that he could feed his family by reaping the wheat of his field or hunting the local wildlife; a time before televisions, computers, and social-media updates; a time where a man earned his respect by the daily dedication to responsibility and practiced humility, not by destroying his neighbor's life or reputation (Romans 12:10); a time when honorable men were anointed by the strength of their character and rose to ascendency through piety (Titus 1:7). But those days were long gone.

The world man had created was one of decadence; deceit; pride and envy; of sloth and fear; lust and gluttony.

They had forgotten how to look toward the heavens (1 Corinthians 2:9). The stars were barely visible at night, and the veil had thickened over their eyes. Even now as we walked amongst them, they were no longer capable of seeing us. Their vacant minds were obstructed by cell-phone screens and RF signals. Their hearts were filled with shame and guilt buried under their desires and selfishness (Galatians 5:19–21). Yet their souls mourn for the bond they lacked through their convictions. And my every essence mourned with them.

The link between man and his Creator had been all but severed through centuries of *human progress*.

"What is to be done?" Gabriel inquired. "The intrinsic value of life has been blurred from their sight. They no longer recognize their inherent meaning."

"The Lord will fulfill His covenant." My response was seemingly less empathetic than intended as I settled my pace on a bus-stop bench.

Across the road stood a clinic, a great darkness emanating from it. This was a place of death. A young woman could be seen through the window, her face hidden under a large summer hat. Her posture was one of impatience, not from the wait but rather from a desperate hope of not being recognized. Her conscience weighed heavily on her but not fully understanding that this choice would haunt her forever.

A man in a white coat entered the room. He muttered something in the girl's direction, his attention fixed on a clipboard held callously in one hand as he scribbled something with the other. He turned and held the door open, and the young girl with a small bump below her bosom followed. The door closed behind them.

"Is the time upon us?" he asked, returning my attention. "Have they really fallen so far that they're beyond redemption? Is there truly no other way?"

"Only He knows, brother," I responded. "Perhaps if we succeed in our endeavor, they may reverse their course."

We turned to see the bus beginning its approach.

"Perhaps," I said, "some of them still remember the flood."

\*\*\*\*\*

Abram stood outside the healer's quarters with his brother Haran pacing back and forth. The cries of Haran's wife could be heard through the sealed entryway.

"Soon, brother. Soon your son will be born, and with him a new generation of God's people will inherit our abundance." Abram's words soothed

Haran's discomfort and eased his worry. "We are truly blessed!"

"You are right, brother," he responded with a reluctant smile.

Suddenly, the cries of pain ceased and were replaced by the cries of a newborn. Haran quickly threw open the entryway, but his jovial smile feigned to a look of horror. The healer had covered the infant with a pitch-black cloth, symbolizing a dark birth.

"What has happened?" Haran cried. "I hear my son's cries, but you've covered him as if he was stillborn."

His perspective shifted to his wife whose body lay concealed under a sheet. She had not survived the birth.

He rushed to her side and began to weep, pounding his hand on the ground beside her. Abram entered and rested his hand sympathetically on Haran's shoulder.

"I'm sorry, brother," he said with remorse.

The healer handed the new father his son. Haran moved the cloth and uncovered the infant's eyes. And they peered deeply at one another.

Haran's cries of sadness became tears of joy as the infant wrapped its tiny hand around his finger. He kissed him and held him close, feeling at any moment that this new light could fade and he would forever be in darkness.

And he prayed.

"Thank you, Lord," Haran said finally. "This boy will do your works as long as I live. Never again will I allow the veil to be pulled before his eyes. My son, my Lot."

*****

It seemed so long ago when I met Abram. After the death of his brother, the responsibility of fatherhood fell to him, and he was proud to accept it. So he took his nephew as his own son, and Lot reciprocated. Abram and his wife, Sarai, had given up hope they'd ever have a child of their own as they had grown mature in age, and Abram had become at peace with their adoption.

Sarai, however, hadn't truly felt fulfilled, having never nursed her husband's seed. And though their love was never in doubt, this contentious issue was often the topic of argument and the call of prayer, making it all the more odd when I arrived.

I rode down early that morning in the twilight before sunrise. Abram was sitting on the tallest hill in Canaan, and as every morning, he was deep in prayer. He opened his eyes and looked up, as if expecting my arrival.

"The sky is especially glorious this morning!" he greeted with sincerity.

"Yes, indeed, my friend. God has blessed this day and with it those who appreciate His many gifts. What is your name, sir, that I might bid you a proper *good morning*?" I asked.

"Abram, my lord. And to whom do I owe the pleasure?" he responded.

"Michael, a name as old as time itself," I said, referencing his ancestor Adam. "Are you here often, Abram? This hill is quite a distance from any settlement nearby."

"Every morning." He closed his eyes and breathed deeply. "My brother and I would play here as children, and since he departed for better company, I gave this hill his name. He was a great man and championed over many mountains but would always find time to worship and taught his son the same. I too love our heavenly Father, and I know His plan is just. So I have prayed here every morning on the back of my brother to be as close to them as possible."

"Indeed again, Abram, God has rewarded him in heaven, and he will reward you as well. In fact, I've come to deliver such a message unto you this morning."

Abram looked surprised, but I suspected a part of him already knew.

"You and your wife, Sarai, will conceive," I continued. "And she will bear you a son."

Abram's face was filled with color, and he jumped up and embraced me. He and his wife were advanced in their age, and the idea of siring an heir seemed more whimsical than myth at that point.

"I can't believe my ears!" he shouted. "God truly does have a sense of humor!"

And together we laughed.

# Chapter Seven

## The Value in Kinship

*THE BREAKS SQUEAKED* AND HYDRAULICS hissed as the bus came to a stop. We had reached the furthest point available before the route reversed, and we decided to depart, stepping out and onto a path leading toward the coast. The sun hung low in the afternoon sky. The soft sounds of the shore could be heard in the distance, and as we approached, the sounds were amplified by gulls and the contagiously innocent laughter of children.

The sight was like an old, torn photograph, beautiful and nostalgic but lacking in an almost undefined way partly due to wear from exposure of the elements and partly due to mental fatigue of the constant struggle to forget.

The children ran up and down the boardwalk, some in their teens, some much younger, their innocence masking their pain.

"Surely, these voices are not those of the wicked." Gabriel observed, resting his hand on the measure.

"What you say is true, Gabriel, and the youth before us carry no true sin but look closer." I nodded in the direction of passersby. "Where is their father? Where is *their* mother? Why are their families incomplete?"

"Perhaps their attendance was impossible," he responded.

"Perhaps, brother. But in the eyes of our Lord, there is but one valid reason their attendance would not be permitted, and we know that's not true for the present examples before us. These children have not lost either parent in life but rather *have* lost them in *spirit*." I made a gesture to prove my point. "His father is working. Her mother is socializing. Their parents have divorced. They are all fractured, divided for the sole purpose of mismanaged priorities."

Gabriel looked upward for a moment, imagining the weight of a relative loss and picturing the vacuum it would create. He turned to me with a confused look, a tear releasing from his eye.

"How does one hold more value in work than in the company of his family? How can a covenant be broken when it's been made before God?"

He paused, overwhelmed by the thought.

"Michael, I...without our Father...without you...the heavens would... I dare not imagine," he stammered.

*****

Gabriel and I approached the end of the short valley from Hedron where earlier that day we were courted by the hospitality of Abraham, a new name gifted from God to Abram for his courageous quest of leadership (Genesis 17:5). Our task could not be hidden from his dexterity, and his communion with God continued past our departure (Genesis 18:16–33).

As we reached the gates of Sodom, we were greeted by a familiar face. Lot was standing guard at the gate near his new home and received us with the same warmth and generosity of that of his uncle. And in the same vein, he recognized our arrival with an ominous suspicion.

"My lords, turn aside to your servant's house, wash your feet, and spend the night. And your journey can continue in the early morning" (Genesis 19:1–2).

His voice wavered slightly. His hospitable nature was pure, but his intent was hidden.

"Our destination is not beyond Sodom but at its square," Gabriel replied.

"I insist!" he responded. "My wife has just begun preparing unleavened bread. Please do not turn away from my lowly offering. Come, feast and be merry."

Gabriel and I shared a glance, knowing we couldn't refuse such an offer of kindness from one of God's true children. So we acquiesced and were humbled by his geniality. And merry it was.

Just as we had decided to turn in, a thunderous sound of treading feet surrounded us with murmurs of profanity echoing throughout. A mob consisting of the whole population of the city had come to Lot's door (Genesis 19:4).

No sooner had I began to wonder when one of them spoke, "Lot!" The voice bellowed. "We know you've taken in new friends. Why not introduce us? We're quite excited to *know* them" (Genesis 19:5).

A volley of laughter erupted, the hungering voices like howling wolves snarling and growling after their prey.

Reluctantly, Lot quickly exited, closing the door behind him.

Standing tall and blocking the entrance, he pleaded, "Please, brothers, don't do this evil. These kind travelers have entrusted me with their safety, and to release them at this hour would bring great shame on my home."

"How dare you judge us, newcomer!" their leader yelled violently. "Look here, boys! He thinks he can just show up in our town and disrespect our customs! Listen, outsider, and listen well. We have a way of living in this city, and it's no place of yours to assume dominion over our etiquette. So open your doors to us, in tolerance, or the fate of your friends will be doubled upon you, bigot!" (Genesis 19:9).

The mob began to inch their way toward him, their faces warped and sickly looking as their inner depravity melted its way to their outward appearance. Their bodies were bending and reshaping into demonic beasts of pure sinful self-indulgence. Lot hadn't realized he was backing away until he ran out of room, putting his body flat against the wall behind him.

Then they swung their weapons in Lot's direction to move, to maim, to murder. Lot covered his face and gritted his teeth. And in that moment, God's will became clear to us, and our errand was confirmed.

Time stopped, and with a nod, Gabriel and I pulled Lot away back inside. And with the light of the Holy Spirit, we threw out our wings, blinding the mob and throwing them back (Genesis 19:10). Screams of violent agony kept them at their knees as they stumbled desperately about the road like injured animals gone feral.

Sheathing my celestial weapons, I turned to Lot.

"Come, Lot! Take your family and flee from this place! But keep the city behind you and don't look back, for God has heard the cries of Sodom, and His judgment is to raze this city from the earth! And we have been sent to extract you and yours so that you might live. The time to take action is upon us. We must make haste!" (Genesis 19:17).

We fought our way through the crowd of hostiles, still emboldened by their insatiable lust for wickedness, and together we ran from Lot's home and continued with urgency until the city was long at our backs.

And the heavens rained fire down on Sodom, striking its inhabitants from history (Genesis 19:24). The heat was so strong that we could feel the annihilation of the city far behind us, and the alluring itch on the backs of our necks proved too enticing for one of our party.

Lot, who was taking the rear of our convoy, looked up as his wife began to turn, and before he could respond, her body hardened to a pillar of salt before his eyes (Genesis 19:26).

He wanted to cry out in anguish, cry out in terror, cry out in sorrow, but he withheld himself, knowing that his daughters could not be allowed to turn, for they too would share in his wife's fate. So he cried silently, gave her coarse cheek a kiss, and continued onward, stricken with grief.

As the night grew deeper, the city became more distant, and the safety of our compatriots was ensured.

"I am sorry, my lords. I was wrong to think I could keep you from the hands of the Sodomites." Even after the hours of travel, Lot had not been able to stop the flow of tears. "And now I have lost my heart and with her my progeny. I have no son to inherit my house, nor have I any reasons for leaving my uncle in the first place."

Lot's heart was filled with longing and regret. And at that moment, I realized Lot would never see Abraham again, nor would he know that his closest kin would soon have a true heir. The only chance he had for an heir of his own had hardened to rock on the pathway out of sin.

And though he would live eternity in heaven, the sins of his house would continue to haunt him still. And my heart wept.

# Chapter Eight

## What Sacrifice Yields

*WE TRAVELED INLAND* FROM THE SANDY beach to the hard concrete of a nearby city. The serene sounds of the ocean were replaced by the chaotic noises of passing cars, animated billboards, and nightclubs. Dusk had taken its claim, and the evening fell upon us.

The lights of the city cascaded over the darkness, emulating day but entombed under night. One could barely smell the air through the dense atmosphere of smog, cigarette smoke, and urine. Gabriel and I shared a glance of shame in recognition of a distant reference.

The outer rim of the city was dystopian, an image of horrific irony surrounding the alluring glimmer of false hope at its center. The highways leading out of the city were worn, barely standing, littered at their bases with makeshift tents and garbage fires. Faces of the destitute huddled for warmth, broken to submission by their feelings of imprisonment. Their shackles consisted of nothing more than their own hands and the works in which they'd been used, surrendered below the precipice of freedom above them, just out of reach.

We paused as we approached a tired old man. His weak body shrouded under tattered rags patched with dusty newspapers beneath intermittent holes and tears. He looked up at us, revealing his long, matted beard, stained from a lifetime of substance abuse. An odd red mole laid square between his brow, unkempt and long forgotten. His leather skin wrinkled and cracked as he narrowed his eyes, attempting to make out the figures standing before him through poor sight that faded long ago.

"Spare some charity for a broken soul?" he begged, lifting his palms in surrender.

I clasped my hands on his. "And what charity might we offer that would ease your suffering?"

"A couple bucks, spare change, anything really. No generosity is too big or too small for me," he responded.

"We have ears that we might listen and life that we might share, but we have no silver to offer."

"No money eh? So you're just as poor as I am! Ha!" He cackled.

"We carry no coin but are quite wealthy, for our fortune is in faith," Gabriel added invitingly (James 2:5).

The old man seemed intrigued by the notion and motioned for us to sit.

"Have a seat, gents! The fire is just warming up." He removed the worn gloves from his hands and wiped the dirt floor, as if clearing the area, and we sat down beside him.

"You're not from around here, are ya?" he asked rhetorically. "I know everyone in this town, and I knew as soon as you came over that you were different." He paused briefly and recollected himself. "Don't mind the floor, been my *bed* for a long time. Ha ha. Must be twenty, maybe thirty years now."

"Have you no home?" I inquired. "Where is your family? Your friends?"

"I have a boy!" He paused for a moment. "Well, I *had* a boy. He's been a *man* for a long time now, much older than I was when he was born. I gave him *all* my money and walked away a long time ago. I knew that he'd be smart and carry on my legacy." He pointed to the center of the city, a towering structure standing like a beacon at its core. "He lives there in the tallest building. He's very successful, yes, sir, a great businessman!"

I shared a look of confusion with Gabriel. The old man's story seemed lacking in practicality, an odd sacrifice with no *real* gain (1 Samuel 15:22).

"Why are you not with him?" I asked. "Even now, he can't be more than a few hours walk from here. Surely there's more to prosperity than affluence" (1 Timothy 6:17).

He seemed uncomfortable and dismissive with the implication.

"Humbug!" He coughed and barked. "That's where you're wrong, my friend! There's *no* higher power in this world than the almighty dollar. That's why I gave everything to my boy. You see? What better way than that to put him on the proper path? Now he never needs to worry about where he goes or where he sleeps or where his next meal will come from. He never needs to bother with fear or doubt or penance. He's been *gifted* with a lack of burden and an absence of responsibility."

He picked up a bottle that lay sideways by his feet and peered into it, as if looking for a ship trapped inside. He reached his index finger as far down the neck as it would go and pulled it out with a *thump* then proceeded to lick it like a dog cleaning the meat off a bone.

"Besides," he continued, "he's far too busy, and that's that as I see it. I've been where he is. I was once a businessman myself with a vagabond father. All he ever did was hold me back! I knew I wouldn't make that mistake with my son, and I *chose* to break the inevitable cycle. So I'm glad for him! What more could any man offer that my son doesn't already have?"

\*\*\*\*\*

The Lord sent me down to Abraham in the early morning after an illuminating visit in a dream. I was to remain cloaked outside of sight but close, as He knew His son would perform His commission despite its trepidatious nature. And Abraham held no pause in fulfilling His task (Genesis 22:1–2).

I watched in concealment as he gathered his men with his son Isaac and loaded his donkey with split wood for the burnt offering to come. I watched as he and his son gave their farewells to Sarah, not wavering for even a moment in their conviction as they departed for Moriah.

Hours passed, and the day broke fully, and they had arrived at their destination. Abraham looked up to see a shaft of light brighter than the sun shining down at the peak of the nearby mountain.

He turned to his men. "Rest here with the donkey. The boy and I will worship there and will return, God willing" (Genesis 22:4–5).

And as they neared His chosen location, curiosity beset the mind of Isaac, and he inquired, "My father, I see we have brought wood and the ingredients for fire, but where is the lamb which is to be offered?" (Genesis 22:7).

"I have faith, my son, and *know* that the Lord Himself will provide the lamb." His response was firm and unwavering (Genesis 22:8).

They continued until they had reached the top. Together they built an altar of the nearby stones and covered it with the wood. The sun had reached its highest point, and the time had come.

Abraham turned to his son. "Isaac, my son, hold up your hands so that I might bind your wrists and feet."

"Where is the lamb, Father?" Isaac responded in terror.

"Have faith, my son." Abraham held firm to his calling. "His will be done!"

Isaac was steadfast and Abraham resolute as the father laid the son on the altar. Together they prayed and gave thanks unto God as Abraham pulled the knife from its sheath and lifted it to the sky.

"I love you, Isaac," cried Abraham.

"I love you, Father," cried Isaac.

And the knife descended. This moment was infinite.

I passed through the veil as I gently laid one hand on the shoulder of Abraham and the other on the knife, stopping its course (Genesis 22:11–12). He paused and looked over at my hand, knowing it was I who he had known and shared in our love for the Lord. But I was gone when he turned, for his attention had been drawn to a nearby thicket where a ram stood waiting, caught by its horns (Genesis 22:13).

He pulled Isaac from the altar and untied him. Abraham collected the ram from the thicket, a cross-shaped section of its horn chipping off and falling at his feet. He tore a piece of cloth from his garment, fashioned a string, and attached it to the cross, making a necklace.

He then tied it around the neck of Isaac and said, "God has delivered us today, and this day is sacred. Remember this cross and carry it all the days of your life. For when your days have reached an end, your son will receive it, and the inheritance God has promised us will continue forever. Amen" (Genesis 22:15–18).

And so God, through Abraham, blessed his son Isaac, and they returned to the altar and fulfilled the sacrifice which the Lord had provided. And again

God blessed him and his seed. For he had not withheld his son from Him.

*****

We entered the dark heart of the city the following morning. A plethora of behemoth buildings were looming over us like foreboding giants. The leviathan of structures brought forth bitter nostalgia of a time long erased, a time of giants, the time of Noah. We readied ourselves in the bodies of men, blending in for the inevitable encounters with them. A feeling of emptiness swept over me as I took their shape, suddenly recognizing my vulnerability, for demons surely haunted this region.

We approached the massive building, colossal letters running down its side, "Y-I-E-L-D," a name belonging to the proprietor of the many rotten businesses and corrupt institutions of the city. We entered and approached the counter. The perfectly polished floors reflected the lobby's ceiling which was no less than twenty feet off the ground. A figure stood at the far end before us like a speck of dust. The wooden chair he sat upon creaked, sliding across the glossy floor as the figure stood and began in our direction. His expensive shoes tap-dancing with echoes in all directions, a smug concierge, a bootlicker by trade. He greeted us with insincerity.

"Good morning, sirs!" he prompted, recognizing the pedigree of our disguise. "Can I help you with anything?"

"We have an appointment with the man of the tower, Mr. Yield. He's been expecting us," Gabriel explained.

"Yes, of course. The elevator on the left will take you directly to his door. Please," he paused arrogantly, "have a great day."

We stepped into the elevator, and the sliding doors closed behind us. As we passed the fortieth floor, the wall we faced became a window, revealing the vile city below, a retreating hellscape of noxious servitude as we climbed higher and higher.

Sixtieth, eightieth, and finally, *ding, ding, ding*.

We arrived at the ninety-ninth floor, the top of the tower.

The doors slid open, and we entered the foyer. Colosseum pillars lined the walls, pointing to a single door at their center. We approached and gave the door a loud knock.

But there was no answer.

We shared a look of concern and tried again then a third time, but the result was the same. Sensing wickedness looming, I peered over at Gabriel who too recognized the dark omen.

Immediately, we liberated ourselves from the bodies of men and stretched out our wings as we stormed into the castle's entry. But our untimely arrival brought no good fortune.

The demon roared from above the body of the dead man below him. Its toothed mouth was long and dark, an incubus finishing its meal. Its forked tail was wrapped tightly around its victim's neck as it stood over its claim defensively.

"Vile beast! You've stolen your last human soul!" Gabriel thundered mightily.

We readied our weapons as the beast took its footing and lunged in my direction.

Its mouth opened down its torso like a volcano. Its sharp teeth were spiraling inward to the dark center where its heart should be.

I narrowly avoided its attack. The feathers of my wings filled the air around us.

Acting swiftly, Gabriel dispatched the demon with a flutter of his wings, slicing the beast in half.

It screamed in agony as its body burnt to ash, leaving behind a putrid smell of damp sulfur.

Then it was gone, and silence gripped the air.

"We are too late, Michael," Gabriel said.

"Yes, brother," I replied, "the Lord's plan has been defiled, and this demon has claimed his soul."

The lifeless body slouched back on the lavish couch. His open eyes rolled back and glassy. A pistol laid clasped in his left hand, smoke rising from the barrel now resting victoriously between his thighs.

"Pity," I said finally. "His influence was all that could change the outcome of this city. He alone had the power to save the lives laid to waste by their addiction to their wickedness, and now that chance has been lost."

And as we turned to exit, an object caught my eye. In his right hand was a picture, old and faded. The image was of a young man holding his infant son. His face was familiar, an odd red mole between his brow.

# CHAPTER NINE

# THE WILL OF GOD

*MANY DAYS HAD PASSED* AND OUR JOUR-
ney was reaching its end. The heavy measure, still
held confidently by my brother, had counted many
worthy, but far more it had not. I had come to the
conclusion that my nervous glances at its number
were only adding to my pessimism, and I would
wait until it was returned to be confronted with His
judgment.

Gabriel, however, seemed not to bat an eye
toward the curiosity that the measure beset. At this
point, it was much safer in his hands.

We landed discreetly in a small town, nothing
but open road for miles surrounding it. It seemed a
quiet place to rest and share in conversation.

The town was buzzing with men, women, and
children, all hard at work and performing their daily
duties with intent and vigor, not a frown or grimace

among them. The simple town was clean and very well organized. Its structures were built no higher than a few stories, namely the schoolhouse and the small church which stood tall in the center of the town.

"Good morning!" said a child passing by on his bicycle, throwing rolled-up newspapers from a large sack that hung over him like a vest.

"Good morning, young man!" Gabriel shouted back.

We continued toward the church. Its short steeple was admirably plain, not held over the town like a tyrant, but standing as a lighthouse, welcoming as sanctuary to those who seek it. The sounds of the congregation inside grew louder as we approached. Hymns of psalms and songs of worship emanated from its walls and overtook us as we entered, claiming our seats in the back.

The pastor stood at the far end of the chapel, his appearance matched those seated behind him. He was not facing away from the congregation but toward a large cross before us. His hands were raised upward in His direction.

The singing came to an end, and he bowed his head.

"Let us pray," he said before turning back. "Lord, we thank you for your many blessings. We work every day to live up to your gifts, and we know we stumble and fall short. We ask that you continue to guide us and grant us the patience we desperately need in our anticipation for your return. Amen" (Proverbs 22:4).

"Amen," we replied, along with the congregation.

The piano started up; then the people stirred and exited. Gabriel and I made our way over to the pastor.

"What a beautiful service," I said, reaching out my hand.

"We are blessed with the Holy Spirit here, and God's good favor has graced us." He received my hand invitingly. "Welcome to our modest town, gentleman. What—may I ask—brings you?"

"We were passing through when we heard the gospel songs," Gabriel replied. "And decided to briefly rest and witness."

"I know a man of God when I see one." The pastor smiled. "If it's rest you need, we've got more than enough space to—"

His words were cut short by a loud crash outside. We quickly made our way through the entry and threw open the doors. A car had crashed over the curb and wrapped into a telephone pole. The man inside was not moving.

In the street lay a boy, rolled papers scattered about around him. His bicycle was wedged behind the rear bumper of the car.

I looked at Gabriel who was holding out the measure, tears flowing down his face. Its number slowly subtracting.

\*\*\*\*\*

Many years passed, and Abraham, after his wife, left the world of men and joined us in heaven. Their earthly bodies were buried side by side (Genesis 25:9–10). Isaac had grown into maturity and married. His wife, Rebekah, beautiful and pure, ensnared Isaac with comfort and security.

They were married almost two decades and found great love and happiness but were unsuccessful in conceiving a child. They loved each other deeply, and Isaac had never known another woman. Rebekah felt unworthy of Isaac, knowing that through him all of God's children on earth were promised, but through her, no son had been carried.

Sensing her discomfort, Isaac joined her in prayer, "Lord, my God, God of my father, I have worshipped you all my life, and I thank you for your everlasting love extended through your works every day. But I am coming upon old age and have no heir to receive your blessings upon my death. Lord,

send us guidance that we might do your will. Amen"
(Genesis 25:21).

*****

That night, Rebekah dreamt of a hilltop sur-
rounded by water. A fissure divided the water into
two sections, one rippling with moving current, the
other glassy and still. In the center of each body of
water stood a man. One was facing toward the sun,
the lake swelling and wrinkling outward from him.
The other was facing away from the sun, admiring
his reflection in the still water.

The sun became eclipsed by the shape of a
massive figure, His feet gently touching the ground
before her. He crouched down to her. His mighty
size was causing the ground to shake and the wind
to roar as He moved, bringing His posture forward
and placing His hand on her shoulder. Falling to
her knees in worship, she lifted her hands upward
toward His towering presence.

The figure spoke thusly, "I have heard your
prayer, and the prayer of your husband, Isaac. His
works and yours bring happiness to his father and
mother who are now with me. Together we are overjoyed and celebrate with every breath you take."

She dared not look up for fear of being blinded,
but with her head bowed, she opened her eyes and

saw her belly was large and with child, much larger however than that of a normal pregnancy. And there was great movement and strain inside it.

"O Lord, if this be your will, why does my child move and struggle so greatly?" she cried.

He responded, "From Isaac, two nations will you carry, for two sons will come from you in one birth. One nation will be stronger than the other as he will inherit my will from his father. The other will presuppose his position as his right of birth, for he will have seniority. And in this way, the younger will supplant the older" (Genesis 25:23).

The rippling water bubbled and shook as a dozen fish jumped all around the man facing the sun. But in contrast, the still water receded, and the man facing away from the sun was left alone in a barren lake.

And she awoke.

\*\*\*\*\*

Esau was a brilliant hunter, born with the strength and dexterity of a wild animal. His burly physique and hairy makeup made him an ideal sportsman, and no game was too big (Genesis 25:27). He carried a necklace around his nape, a gift handed down from his father, Isaac, in remembrance of a sacrifice made by his grandfather, Abraham, before God.

But sacrifice was alien to Esau. He had not wanted for the spoils of this world, for to desire would at first require him to be challenged, and there was no physical challenge that he could not easily overcome. This would be his downfall.

His twin brother, Jacob, was much simpler. He had no such gift of strength nor endowment of skill and was not favored by any other than his mother. But he had an affinity for manipulation and often put his ingenuity to practice on Esau.

The brothers would often bicker and fight with one another, but with Esau clearly possessing the upper hand physically, Rebekah would often intervene, revealing her favoritism (Genesis 25:28). This would only increase their rift ultimately.

One day, when Esau returned home from a long hunt, covered in trophy skins of elk and boar, he was greeted by the aroma of stew wafting through their home. He was tired from the long day and very hungry.

"What is this sweet smell you are cooking?" he asked.

"It should be no worry of yours," Jacob replied annoyingly. "As I have prepared it for myself."

"Do not be selfish, brother! Allow me a taste. I am famished!" Esau responded forcefully.

"Mmmm, my favorite! Red-lentil stew. You are quite fond of it too, as I recall," Jacob continued, antagonistically fanning the smoke toward his face (Genesis 25:30).

"Come, brother, be not mine enemy." Esau was now attempting to persuade Jacob. "Have your pick of my trophies, a fair trade."

Sensing the upper hand, Jacob responded, "But I too am hungry, and what good will your hides do *me*?"

"What do you want? Take anything, please!"

Jacob paused his stirring of the stew and peered at his brother wickedly.

"Anything?"

Esau's patience was wearing thin. "I will have no more of this quarrel! Take my offer, or I shall take my leave!"

He turned to exit.

"Your birthright," Jacob said slyly (Genesis 25:31).

Esau stopped dead in his tracks. "What?"

"Relinquish your inheritance unto me," Jacob continued. "And you shall receive all I have prepared."

Esau took a step back and clutched the necklace on his chest, realizing that his father had endowed it to him, and like his father before him, he had never removed it. He paused to think about the value but was overcome by his hunger.

"So be it!" he replied through frustration. "What good is a birthright if I die of starvation!" (Genesis 25:32).

He ripped the yoke from his neck and hurled it at Jacob, striking him on the forehead and falling to the floor.

Jacob knelt down and retrieved the necklace from his feet. He stood up and walked to the doorway (Genesis 25:34).

"Enjoy, brother," he said as he exited. "A fair trade indeed."

*****

Isaac lay patiently in bed for Rebekah to return. He had sent her for water but had begun to regret it as he grew weaker with each passing moment.

Esau entered the room in haste, a concerned look on his face.

"Father, you are ill?" he cried.

Isaac had grown blind in old age, and the rest of his senses followed quickly thereafter.

"Esau? Is that you?"

"I am here. Mother will return shortly with the water." He reassured his father.

"My son, I am old, and my time is short. Take your bow and quiver and hunt for me a great venison. Then prepare my final meal. When all is done,

I will bless you as my father blessed me." Isaac's words were soft and tired through his quick breaths (Genesis 27:2–4).

"Yes, father, at once!" Esau replied, quickly running out the doorway.

Rebekah had just returned as Esau was making his exit, and she knew Isaac would not have long.

She ran to Jacob, "My son, you haven't much time. You must receive your father's blessing before God. Quickly, run to the flock and bring back two choice goats. Then I will make him his favorite meal, and you will deliver it to him" (Genesis 27:5–10).

"But, Mother," he responded, "isn't the blessing intended for Esau? I know he is arrogant, but he loves our father. Suppose I am the last to speak to him, wouldn't I be cursed rather than blessed?"

Rebekah put her hand on his. "Your curse has always been and will always be on me, my son" (Genesis 27:13).

He ran out and returned shortly; then together, Jacob and his mother made Isaac's favorite meal and brought it to his bedside all while Esau was still hunting.

"My love, my husband, your son has returned and prepared for you your favorite meal." Rebekah's voice wavered gently as she waved her hand at Jacob. "Come in, Esau, and sit with your father so that he will bless you."

"My son, what great skill you possess to have returned so quickly," Isaac said, surprised.

Rebekah threw a skin of one of the prepared goats on Jacob then pulled Esau's clothes over him and gave a wink at her son. Jacob was confused, but he trusted his mother and played along.

"Y-yes, father," Jacob said as he sat down beside Isaac, "the Lord your God has worked it out for me" (Genesis 27:19–23).

Isaac squinted his failed eyes and reached out his hand to touch his son. "Your voice is like Jacob, but your skin is like Esau." He took a deep breath. "My eyes have failed me in my old age, but my nose, though weak, does not lie. I know your scent my son" (Genesis 27:27).

Jacob darted a look at his mother who was standing at the doorway. She smiled back, and Jacob realized his normal clean scent was overpowered by the smell of his brother's clothes.

"Ah, the smell of my son is like the smell of a field that the Lord has blessed," Isaac continued. "May God give to you from the dew of the sky and the richness of the land an abundance of grain and new wine. May people serve you and nations bow down to you. May you be master over your brothers, and may your mother's sons bow down to you. Those who curse you will be cursed, and those that bless you will be blessed" (Genesis 27:28–29).

Jacob kissed the forehead of his father and exited, passing his brother in the doorway. Their eyes met for an instant, lasting an eternity then breaking as he disappeared into the dark field.

I'll never forget how Esau's cries rippled through the veil and reached my ears that night (Genesis 27:34).

*****

We entered the local inn as the sun began to set, the entryway split in three directions. To the left was the dining area with a large table filling the center. To the right was a living area with couches, games, and the warmth and inviting comfort of a crackling fireplace. Directly in front of us was a staircase leading up to the rooms. The rarity of an outside visitor made for a wealth of vacancy, but the silence gripping the air was the result of the tragic events that unfolded earlier in the day.

A young woman rounded the corner from the dining room, jumping in shock as she had not heard us enter.

"Oh! My apologies," she curtsied. "I didn't know we had guests. You must be the visitors our pastor mentioned. Please make yourselves comfortable and join us for dinner."

"We'd be honored. Thank you," Gabriel replied.

We went upstairs and prepared our beds then cleaned our feet and hands before returning to the dinner table.

The young woman had set the meal and stood patiently awaiting at the right-hand seat to the head of the table. Her children sat in their respective seats—two boys, eighteen and eleven; two girls, sixteen and nine. Their heads were bowed in prayer. We watched in admiration, not fully grasping the situation.

"Have a seat and join us in saying grace," she said softly.

"Is your husband not home? Will he be joining us?" I asked.

She turned to hide her tears from her children. "I'm sorry, but he was in an accident today, and we're not sure if he's going to make it."

"I'm very sorry," I said regretfully. "He has a beautiful family."

We sat and bowed our heads.

"Dear heavenly Father," she began, "we thank you for this meal and the kindness of our community. Please continue to watch over us with your loving grace and my children's father. Keep him close and grant him peace, if You must take him. Please, Lord, grant your mercy over the boy who now lies in a coma and give comfort to his family who sits in wait by his side. We ask in the name of Jesus. Amen."

The somber air lingered thickly over the table as the children picked and poked at their food, sniffing and sobbing gently under their collective cloud of sadness.

*****

Jacob walked alone through the empty valley on his way to Haran. His brother's distraught turned quickly to vengeance, and their mother sent him away for fear of Esau exacting his murderous plans (Genesis 27:41–45).

Terror gripped Jacob, and he fled with haste and regret, for he knew what he had done.

The day had grown dark, and Jacob was several days out on his journey. Tired and worn, he entered a cave for sanctuary from the night (Genesis 28:11). The cave curved around, revealing a chamber at its center, a large hole in the ceiling providing ample moonlight encircled by a portrait of stars.

An alter of stones sat firmly in the umbra of illumination, with grass and moss growing between them. He grabbed one of them which had a groove lain on its top, perfect for a man's head to lay on. So he did, and before he knew it, he was asleep.

*****

A rushing sound of wind tickled his ears as he stood waist high in tall grass. He opened his eyes and realized he was outside the cave and could see it a short distance away, the moonlight still illuminating its canopy.

Suddenly, the moon began to turn orange in color, and the stars around it faded as it grew brighter, becoming like daylight. Then a tear split the moon horizontally, and the sky receded like a scroll, revealing a bright light emanating from behind it. The light pierced downward into the cave and took the shape of a spiraling staircase (Genesis 28:12).

Jacob was still with amazement, gazing childishly at the angels sitting, walking, flying up and down the stairs. Our eyes met briefly as he watched me glide down on my way to earth for an (unrelated) errand, but that's another story. I didn't keep his attention long, for at the top of the staircase stood the Lord, gripping it with His right hand (Genesis 28:13).

And He spoke, "Jacob, I am the God of your father, Isaac, and his father, Abraham. Your mother has done according to my will, and you have received your father's blessing. The land you sleep on is the land I promised your father's father, and where he proved himself to me, and I now promise it to you and your seed. Your offspring will be like the dust of the earth and will spread outward in all directions from here. And all who live on this land and bless you will in return be blessed, for I will be with you" (Genesis 28:14–15).

Then the sky sealed with a loud boom, waking him from his dream. Jumping to his feet, he looked around in the darkness, back to reality, back to the cave. He could almost still feel the warmth of the staircase on the dirt beneath his feet (Genesis 28:16–17).

\*\*\*\*\*

His journey continued for another day until he came upon a field with a watering well surrounded by sheep. A woman sprung up from amongst them, young and beautiful, and caught his eye immediately.

"What land is this?" he inquired.

"This is Haran, the land of my father's father," she replied (Genesis 29:4).

"I come searching for Laban, my uncle. Might you know him?" he asked.

"Yes, he is my father. And who might you be?"

"I am Jacob, son of Isaac and Rebekah. Your father is my mother's brother. I wish to request an audience with him."

Her face lit up with a bright smile, and she ran to Jacob, throwing her arms around him. He flustered and froze with embarrassment in response (Genesis 29:11–12).

"I'll bring him at once!" And she ran off.

He sat at the mouth of the well and pondered, the smell of her hair and the feel of her soft skin still strong in his memory. He was smitten.

Before he knew it, she had returned, her father at her side.

"Jacob! My nephew!" Laban shouted jovially. "Welcome to my land! Come and feast. We have much to discuss."

Jacob stood to meet his uncle who grabbed and hugged him tightly. They exchanged pleasantries and headed to Laban's home (Genesis 29:13–14).

Jacob enjoyed the hospitality of his uncle for a month before Laban took issue. Seeing as how Jacob had no real skill in labor, Laban and his daughter Rachel helped to educate him in the works of shepherding, and soon he carried his weight.

Laban was no fool. He recognized the shared affection between Jacob and Rachel, and a deal was made.

"I will work for you seven years," Jacob bargained. "And in return, I ask for your daughter's hand" (Genesis 29:18).

"What better suiter for my daughter than you, my boy?" Laban agreed. "I possess no interest in wedding my daughters to a stranger."

Rachel was the second born of Laban's daughters. The oldest, Leah, was not as fair and had no real spirit of youth in her eyes (Genesis 29:17). As the years passed, Laban took concern in her lack of male affection.

The seven years came and went, and finally, the day had come.

Jacob sent for Rachel, and that night in the darkness, they laid together.

Or so he thought.

When morning broke, Jacob turned to his wife who lay beside him, and behold, it was not Rachel but Leah. He had been deceived (Genesis 29:25).

He quickly ran out and confronted Laban, "I was to have Rachel as my wife! You have forced my hand unto sin having lain with Leah whom I do not love."

"It is not our custom to marry the latter born before the first," he responded slyly. "If you wish the hand of Rachel also, I propose a renewal of our contract. Seven more years and she is yours."

Jacob's love for Rachel exceeded his feelings of betrayal, and though frustrated, he acquiesced (Genesis 29:26–27).

The years went quickly yet again as every passing day brought him closer to his love. And at the completion of the renewed bargain, Jacob and Rachel were finally together.

They loved each other greatly but had no luck in conceiving a child. Leah, however, had no such problem, for God looked upon her shame with kindness and begat four sons from Jacob (Genesis 29:31–35).

Reuben was the first; so named by Leah, for God had seen her affliction. The second, Simeon, was so named, for God had heard her prayers. The third, Levi, was so named as Leah had hoped his birth would bring union between her and her husband. The forth, Judah, was so named as praise unto God.

Rachel, feeling envious of her sister and her ability to carry, sent her servant unto Jacob as her proxy, and she had two more sons (Genesis 30:1–8).

Dan was so named for God's judgment unto Rachel. And Naphtali was so named for the ongoing struggle between the sisters.

But the hostility would continue, and Leah too sent her servant to Jacob as a proxy and begat two more sons (Genesis 30:9–13).

The first, Gad, was so named for Leah's good fortune, and the second, Asher, was so named for the happiness he brought with his birth.

But over time, this only increased Leah's shame, and with the help of a mandrake, a strong aphrodisiac, she conceived yet again, two more sons and a daughter (Genesis 30:16–21).

Issachar, the first, was so named for Leah's recompense. Zebulun, the second, was so named for Leah's dwelling on her shame. And finally, Dinah was so named for the peace she brought to Leah.

Once peace had been attained between the sisters and their husband, God opened Rachel's womb, and she begot her first son. And she named him Joseph, for their wealth increased from that day forward (Genesis 30:22–24).

For the next six years, Jacob worked for the opportunity to escape his dependency from his uncle, and so he made another bargain.

"I will take the speckled and spotted sheep from amongst your herd as payment and be on my way," Jacob said. "From this day on, if any of my sheep stand on your land, you shall claim them as your own" (Genesis 30:25–34).

Laban agreed, and Jacob took his wives and their servants, his sons and daughter, and all their sheep and made their way back to the land of his father, Isaac.

After many years, a final son would be born unto Rachel, and with his birth spell out another messianic prophecy of the Son of Man:

*Behold a Son* comes *hearkening!* A *union* through *praise* and *judgment* of our *struggle*. But we are *fortunate* and we are *blessed* as our *reward*, given through *shame*, grants *peace* and *vindication* as *He will increase* as the *Son of the right hand.*

*****

For twenty years, Jacob worked for his uncle, fourteen for Rachel and Leah and six for ownership of the flock. And it was upon reflection that he recognized his misdeeds to Esau. But having amassed great wealth through the blessings of the Lord, he hoped and longed for reconciliation with his brother (Genesis 31).

So he sent forth a messenger party to inform Esau of his return saying, "Forgive me, brother, for I have sinned against you. I bring an offering unto you that you might have grace in your heart and find kindness in the sight of me" (Genesis 32:3–5).

The messengers returned and told Jacob, "Esau is coming to meet you, and he brings with him an army of four hundred men" (Genesis 32:6).

Jacob, fearing for his family, sent his servants with all his wealth forward to meet his brother. He then hid his family in a separate party along the valley and waited alone (Genesis 32:21–23).

That night, on my way to Job, I happened to chance upon Jacob who restlessly awaited his fate. I hadn't intended on meeting with him but somehow misjudged his tenacity. By the time I realized he had seen me, my stealth had already been compromised.

Thinking of me as his assassin, he lunged and tackled my body to the ground.

I recovered only long enough to be grappled again, his unyielding courage strengthening him. Never had I wrestled so tryingly with a son of Adam.

We struggled and flexed, pushed and pulled, twisted and bent, but as the hours passed, he would not yield (Genesis 32:24). Like a father rolling with his son, I knew I couldn't use my true strength, and somehow, he used this as a weakness against me.

So long had we contended that the day began to break. Knowing I could be held up no longer, I touched the hollow of his thigh, shrinking the tendon and dislocating it from the joint (Genesis 32:25).

Jacob cried out in pain but still kept his hold firm on my wrist. Though he would not win, it became clear that he would not surrender.

"You have fought valiantly! I yield! The morning is here, and I must be on my way, for I am late in my errand," I said (Genesis 32:26).

"Please, my Lord," he responded, "I am awaiting in fear for the fate my brother has designed for me. I have wronged him greatly in my early life and can offer no true justice to him that might still his vengeful heart."

His confusion was understandable and brought a smile to my face. My appearance to those who have never known me bears a striking resemblance to the face of Adam, and with a deep breath, I looked toward the sky. The Lord whispered in my ear, and I remembered my namesake and thought, *For who is like God?*

"What is your name?" I asked.

"Jacob," he responded, "son of Isaac, son of Abraham."

I should have known hours ago from the strength of his determination that he was of the line of Abraham. I should have recognized his zeal and fortitude and remembered why God shows His favor among men. Jacob was none other than one of the children of His chosen. And I had contended with him all night under the witness of our Lord to deliver His personal message.

"Jacob," I responded, "you possess the power of a prince, and your strength and will are unmatched on this earth. You shall no longer be called Jacob, for your supplanting has been usurped. You shall be known as Israel, for you have prevailed against the mighty" (Genesis 32:28).

And with the Lord's blessing upon him, he released me, and I continued my journey, quickly vanishing as Israel turned to face his brother.

Esau approached with his army and halted their pace before his kin. Israel dropped to his knees in forgiveness and begged at his feet. Esau not only held a lack of contempt but was overjoyed at the sight of his long-lost brother. And with tears in their eyes, they embraced one another in reconciliation (Genesis 33:1–4).

*****

The whole town was gripped with shock, still confused about how the child survived and not a scratch on his body. The driver had sustained a massive brain aneurysm, but his soul had left his body before his car hit the boy and struck the telephone pole.

There were flowers laid with pictures of the man at the place of impact. He was loved by many here.

We paid our respects and decided to depart. The pastor was waiting for us at the edge of the city, a newspaper in his hand.

"So sorry you did not have the chance to meet our brother," he said. "He was a great man and will be greeted with warmth in heaven."

"Indeed, my friend," Gabriel replied.

"But his tragic end was not without providence." He paused and opened the newspaper then handed it to me. "A parting gift of witness for my new friends."

I turned the paper to read the headline, "Man's fateful death reveals boy's bad heart. Transplant saves his life."

# CHAPTER TEN

## DREAMS AND PROVIDENCE

*JOSEPH LAY COMFORTABLY* IN THE SHADE of a tree, watching over the herd. He had forgotten the importance of this particular day and performed his duties like any other.

"Joseph!" called the voice of his father.

He jumped up and followed it to the back side of Israel's house.

"Yes, father, here I am," Joseph said as he entered.

"Do you know what today is, my son? It is my favorite day of the year for the last seventeen years [Genesis 37:2], the day you were born," Israel added with a smile.

"Very funny, Father," Joseph responded dismissively. "Surely, Reuben's birthday would be your favorite, if you can make such a distinction."

Israel looked at his son in the eye with an honesty only he would recognize, paused, and shot him a wink. Then he turned to reveal the loom behind him, oddly colored balls of wool strewn about around it. Draped over the loom was a long coat radiantly glowing with all the colors of the rainbow (Genesis 37:3). Magnificent and beautiful, embroidered in its center with a cross-shaped fragment, it was handed down from father to son as an inheritance.

"My gift to you, my favorite son, on the anniversary of your birth."

*****

Joseph's older brothers were always jealous of him (Genesis 37:4), even more than their youngest brother Benjamin, whose birth Rachel did not survive (Genesis 35:16-19). Out of all his wives, Israel had only really loved Rachel, and of all of his thirteen children, Joseph was the first of hers to carry.

It was also true that God showed him favor, for he would often have wonderful dreams that he could recite in great detail (Genesis 37:5), a skill that he had developed well enough to find messages hidden within. All the tribes of the nearby lands would come to him in search for meaning, and he would deliver prophecies unto them through his interpretations.

As the years progressed, his brothers' envy turned to hatred, and their anger made them spiteful.

One day, Israel sent Joseph out to pasture to help his brothers with the herd (Genesis 37:13–14). The flock often ventured to an old, dried-up well on the backside of the prairie, out of sight from home. And he met them there as his father had instructed. The night before, Joseph had a dream and came with excitement to share it with his siblings.

"Brothers, I had another dream last night!" he described. "I was standing like a giant atop a mountain of grain. Above me, the moon, the sun, and eleven stars bowed to me like reeds in the wind" (Genesis 37:9).

"What dream is this?" they responded maliciously. "You expect us, your old father, and your dead mother to bow before you? You wish to rule over us?" (Genesis 37:10–11).

Judah laughed and teased Joseph, "Look, brothers, at our flamboyant ruler and his colorful coat!"

His brothers bellowed with obnoxious laughter and shoved him viciously like a pack of feral hyenas taunting their prey.

Joseph lost his footing and stumbled into the dried-up well. His coat caught the mouth of the pit, and he clung to it for his life, hoping his brothers would help.

Instead, they continued to laugh, and the coat began to tear. Before he could respond, the coat ripped in half, and he fell to the bottom (Genesis 37:23–24).

Feeling bruised but not broken, he lifted himself to his feet. The well was too deep to climb out of on his own. He was stuck.

"Brothers! Help me!" he cried out.

The sun beat down on him from the mouth of the well, and through the whistling wind, he could hear his brothers whispering, eleven round silhouettes peering down at him, and one by one they left. And he was alone, clutching despairingly what remained of his torn heirloom.

Hours passed, and just as Joseph began to give up hope, a rope dropped in and touched the ground at his feet. He wiped the tears from his face and grabbed hold.

*Freedom!* he thought.

But no sooner had he reached the top than his feet and hands were bound, and his captives threw him into a cage attached to a mule (Genesis 37:28).

\*\*\*\*\*

The time had come for our return. These forty days and forty nights were hard for us, and although we witnessed incredible things, the overall journey had impacted us both beyond measure. Needless to say, we were ready to leave.

The golden roads and crystal rivers flashed brilliantly beneath us as we made our final approach.

*What will He decide?* I thought. *What is left to decide? These people are fallen, born unto sin, repeating the same atrocities and abominations over and over. Many are righteous. It's true, but far more are wicked. Such is their curse. Perhaps the time has come, the final hour. Perhaps the trumpets will finally blow, and war will follow. Perhaps—*

My thoughts were broken by Gabriel who handed the measure back to me. Its burden was seemingly heavier than I remembered.

We landed before the throne and knelt.

"My sons, you have returned so soon," said the Lord jokingly. "Time has a way of vanishing by when one is at peace."

I wasn't ready to smile.

"My Lord, we have done what you asked," I started. "We have travelled all across the earth and returned with your measure."

I lifted it high above my bowed head, straining in the hopes he would lift the burden from me.

"You have witnessed many things these past weeks," the Lord continued. "Many faces have you looked on, and many hearts have you touched. What say you of My world's condition?"

The only thing I was more unprepared for in this moment than this question was the answer. My hope in mankind had never been more in question than at this moment, and I didn't know how to respond.

"Lord," I began, "your world is in disarray. Not since the days of Noah have I seen such horrors and betrayals. Their leaders are corrupt. Their laws are unjust. Their temples are desecrated daily. Their false gods are innumerable, and they don't even know they're worshiping them! They celebrate sin and denigrate innocence. They run toward the lies of the moment to escape the truth in their future. Your world's condition is one of disrepair by the very humans who inhabit it, all performing day in and day out the errors of the past! It's fallen, my Lord. Their world is beyond redemption!"

"Michael!" shouted Gabriel, stopping me from continuing.

And like waking from a deep dream, I realized I was no longer kneeling but standing before the feet of God. The measure was still held firmly but no longer outstretched in submission; instead it was clasped in my hardened fist like the hilt of a mighty sword. I peered over its gold reflective surface and saw the eyes of my former brother, Lucifer, burning with anger and vengeance. In that moment, I understood him more than ever.

\*\*\*\*\*

Days became weeks, and weeks became months until Joseph in his captivity could no longer remember how long ago he was sold into his slavery. All he knew was that he must be strong, and he must not give up hope.

And so he prayed in silence.

Just then the door to the dungeon flew open, and he was quickly pulled out, thrown into a bath, and shaved. Before he knew what was going on, he was standing before the pharaoh (Genesis 41:14).

"Hebrew," spoke the pharaoh, "my chief butler has informed me that you have a powerful gift of interpretation, specifically the interpretation of dreams. Is this true?" (Genesis 41:15).

"Yes, but it is not I. It is God who gives the answer," Joseph replied (Genesis 41:16), fearful that with one wrong word, pharaoh would have him executed.

"I have searched my kingdom high and low to find one such as yourself," pharaoh continued. "I have had a powerful dream, one in which has not left me since the night it first appeared. If you can tell me the meaning of this dream, I will release you from servitude."

Joseph paused and reflected pharaoh's offer, knowing this moment would mean the difference between freedom and death. And so he prayed again in silence.

He lifted his eyes back to pharaoh and gave a nod of agreement.

*****

Pharaoh stood along the bank of a river, its reflective surface mirroring the sky above. Suddenly, the river began to ripple, and out of the water came seven herds of cows one after the other, healthy and fat. They collected in a nearby meadow and fed.

Before the water could rest, there came seven more herds of cows; this group were thin and dying. They followed the first group to the meadow but did not feed on the grain. Rather they devoured the healthy cows and were not nourished. Then they turned to pharaoh, and with loud cries, they dropped and died.

He covered his face to hide from the horror. And when he looked, he was no longer there but in an empty field.

He looked around and spotted a small bulb a few feet away. He knelt down beside to examine it. All at once, seven ears of corn shot up from the ground in one stalk, knocking pharaoh on his back. He reached out and ran his finger along the golden-yellow surface; these seven were full and good.

Then a mighty wind from the east blasted the stalk. And before pharaoh's eyes, the stalk had snapped and withered, with nothing remaining but thin and dead ears (Genesis 41:17–24).

*****

Joseph could see clearly the concern in pharaoh's eyes. This was a message from God.

"Your dream is a warning of what God has planned and is even now about to bring upon us," he said, breaking the silence. "The seven good herds of cows are seven years, and the seven good ears of corn are seven years. The seven dying herds are seven years, and the seven bad ears are seven years" (Genesis 41:25–32).

"But what does it mean?" inquired pharaoh.

Joseph swallowed heavily and continued, "There are coming seven years of abundance throughout Egypt. But there are coming seven years of famine after them. The seven years of abundance will bring apathy to the people, and the seven years of famine will consume everything. This is why the message was told twice in your dream. God is telling you what is coming."

"Is there nothing we can do to avoid this?" inquired pharaoh.

"This is God's will. It cannot be stopped," replied Joseph confidently. "However, it can be survived."

Pharaoh's eyes met Joseph's with curious anticipation.

"If pharaoh was to find a wise and noble man," he continued, "and appoint this man to collect a fifth of the excess during each of the seven years of abundance and then store this food for use during the seven years of famine, Egypt will survive" (Genesis 41:33–36).

"What brilliance!" cried pharaoh. "The spirit of God dwells within you, Joseph. And since God has shown all this to you, there can be no one wiser than you" (Genesis 41:38–39).

Pharaoh approached Joseph and rested his arm on his shoulder.

"That is why I'm going to give this responsibility to you," he continued. "To do this job, you will need authority. I hereby make you second in command, answering solely to me" (Genesis 41:40).

A double-edged sword had befallen Joseph. He would have great power but would have to claim even greater responsibility.

*****

I dropped the measure from my hand. I could no longer bear the burden.

"Lord, I'm not worthy of your presence!" I started. "I feel an anger unlike any other. I cannot understand why man inevitably arrives at self-destruction. It's burning my soul like fire!"

A breath of air like a soft typhoon brushed over me as God began to speak.

"Be calm, Michael," he responded, throwing me off balance with comfort and freeing me from my torment. Then turning his attention to my brother, He said, "Gabriel will take you to rest. When you are ready with your answer, then return to me."

And before I knew it, I was asleep.

\*\*\*\*\*

The skies were ablaze with furious delicacy and vibrant tranquility as stars whipped around my vision. Something had changed. I couldn't control it.

The dreams of angels are different from the dreams of men. My dreams can be a lifetime in length. I am born; I am free; I worship the Lord; I die; not always in that order and not always the latter. Time is a dimension in which we exist inside and *outside* of. And our dreams can often manifest physically, for instance, when a star is born or a black hole devours a galaxy. But because our existence is both in and out of time, the dream has the ability to *exceed* the sleep. And if we weren't immortal, the dream could likely exceed the *dreamer*.

But this dream was unlike any I've had before. This dream took me between time neither inside nor out. I could not change anything, yet I could not leave. And as the stars slowed their firing across the sky, I realized that they were moving backward rather than forward. And when they finally stopped, I was standing on the earth again.

*What was I doing here? Why couldn't I leave?*

And as those questions racked my mind, it became clear where and when I was. The famine was everywhere.

\*\*\*\*\*

The famine had come upon the land of Egypt, just as God had warned. Luckily, Joseph and pharaoh had heeded His warning, and their preparation was keeping Egypt alive. But there were some outside of Egypt that were not warned of this coming disaster, among them Israel and his sons and daughter (Genesis 41:53–57).

Israel had heard of Egypt's survival during these last few years and sent ten of his sons to buy corn, leaving only Benjamin behind in case of the worst occurring (Genesis 42:1–5).

When the ten sons of Israel reached Egypt, they knelt before Joseph and did not recognize him (Genesis 42:6–8). Wrought with spite, he used this opportunity to show revenge on his brethren who many years ago had left him for dead, only to sell him into slavery for twenty pieces of silver.

"Where have you come from?" Joseph inquired.

"From the land of Canaan. We wish to purchase food," they responded.

"We have many enemies beyond our borders and in the land of Canaan," Joseph continued. "How do I know you are not spies, only seeking to return to your masters with information on the effect of our famine?" (Genesis 42:9).

"No, my lord," they responded, "we, your servants, have only come for food. We are all brothers from one man, twelve in all. The youngest of us is with our father. The other is gone" (Genesis 42:13).

Their words were like daggers to Joseph's heart. But he could not show them his true emotion. He missed his brother Benjamin and was always concerned that his fate would match his own. If his brothers could perform such horrible acts once, on their father's favorite son, they could do it again.

"Very well," Joseph started, "to show proof of your story and validate your claims, one of you must stay. Those that leave are to return with your absent brother" (Genesis 42:19–24).

They agreed, collected the food, and headed home, leaving only Simeon behind.

But upon their return, they realized their money was still with them, and they had not paid for their food (Genesis 42:27–28). Their fear was immeasurable, knowing they must return with Benjamin also. Through much debate with Israel, the ten brothers again made their way to Egypt. Only this time, they were greeted with hospitality.

Joseph put them up but rejected their reimbursement, saying, "We have your money." Then he reunited them with Simeon and asked them to join him for lunch (Genesis 43:16–25).

Several times Joseph would leave to his bedchambers and cry after laying eyes on his brother Benjamin. It had been so long that he could hardly recognize him, and Benjamin couldn't at all. This emotion created a fire in Joseph, and so he plotted again.

He instructed his servant to hide his silver cup in the belongings of the youngest brother, then upon discovery of its absence, force his brothers into condemning Benjamin to servitude. And his servant did as instructed (Genesis 44:2).

However, once the trap was sprung, the reaction from Joseph's brothers was far from what he had expected.

"Please, my lord," said Judah, "we cannot return to our father without our brother Benjamin. He is the last of two sons from our father's wife Rachel whom he loved more than any. If we were to return without him, our father would die from grief. Please let me stay in his place if only to save my father from heartache" (Genesis 44:18–34).

At this, Joseph could no longer keep his identity secret. How different Judah was from the man who sold him away. The love his brother had shown for their father was staggering, and he knew he must come clean.

"I am Joseph, your brother!" he proclaimed, holding high the cross-shaped heirloom from his father. "The same brother whom you sold into slavery, the same brother whom even now you think dead. Does our father yet live?" (Genesis 45:3).

Paralyzed with shock, his brothers didn't know whether to be overjoyed or terrified of what this meant. Their brother, whom they had stripped of his beautiful coat and left for dead whom they had sold into slavery and lied to their father about his death, was not only alive but the most powerful man in Egypt under pharaoh. But luckily for them, Joseph was more than ready to forgive.

He ran to Benjamin, and they hugged and cried. Then one by one, he hugged and cried with the others. So overjoyed were they to be reunited (Genesis 45:14–15).

"Joseph," asked Judah, "how can we ever deserve your forgiveness when what we did to you is unforgivable?"

Joseph only smiled. "Brother, if not for what happened, I would never have been in the prison. If I were never in the prison, I would never have been able to interpret pharaoh's dream. If I were never able to interpret pharaoh's dream, all of Egypt would've been lost."

They looked on at him in confusion.

"Brothers," he continued, "it was not you who threw me in the well, nor was it you who sold me into slavery. It was God" (Genesis 45:7–8).

*****

I awoke in my bed with new clarity. Not only did I realize the error of my ways but was overwhelmed with the feeling of comfort by way of my new understanding.

This state of mind wasn't reached by my own accord but came from the mouth of a man, a man named Joseph, who I was fortunate to see come to give God the glory of not only his life's greatest moments but also those of greatest hardship. This man was able to see through the noise of vengeance and spite, hurt and anger, fear and dread and trust through faith of our heavenly Father's will.

Not only was I humbled by Joseph's words, I was reminded of the grace, glory, and wisdom of the almighty God. Through Him comes everything—good, bad, or otherwise. I finally had my answer.

At this moment, I realized I was not alone. There sitting next to me was the Lamb of God, the Word, God Himself made flesh.

And He spoke, "Now you understand. You were not sent to the earth for any purpose of man but for your own understanding and reflection. It is true. They are a fallen creation, but their condition, whether good or bad, is the divine will of God. It is true that they possess free will and can do wonderful and terrible things, but only through their freedom can those with eyes to see and ears to hear be wed with truth and attain the gift of salvation. This journey you've been tasked with was not to discover the damning qualities of man but to remember the grace of God."

"I understand," I responded. "But why now? I see how my former brother became the monster that he is. I see that temptation awaits those who put themselves upon the seat of judgment. But why wait until now to show me?"

"This is not the end of your story, Michael. This is only the beginning."

He lifted his hands to my eyes; in them rested the measure. Only now the measure was no longer a rod but a golden strap, a belt.

It was then that I truly understood.

The rod can be a useful tool of correction (Proverbs 10:13, 26:3). In the hand of a shepherd, it could be used to guide his flock, or in the hand of a rider, it can keep his steed on the narrow path. But to gird up one's garments with a belt is to attach the most important pieces necessary to maintaining our defenses and holding up our strengths. Without this foundational piece of armor, we could hold to nothing of substance. We would be exposed, and ultimately we could not testify or align ourselves with Truth (John 14:6, 14:17, 2 Timothy 4:3–4).

And as my eyes began to fill with tears, the belt began to glow:

144,000

# About the Author

RICHARD CAPUTO WAS born and raised in Southern California. For the past thirteen years, he worked in the film industry. Always a creative person, this book is the fruit of his embarking on another artistic adventure. His writing style is both intelligent and thought-provoking, and has become a pursuit of passion in his walk with God.

His weekly Christian podcast, Counting The Days (anchor.fm/richard-caputo), covers many Biblical studies while promoting the gospel to anyone who may be searching, and can be found across all podcasting platforms as well as YouTube. Richard is currently living in Texas.

CPSIA information can be obtained
at www.ICGtesting.com
Printed in the USA
LVHW012031290321
682890LV00002B/118